All Night Long

By Melody Mayer

The Nannies
Friends with Benefits
Have to Have It
Tainted Love
All Night Long

All Night Long

by Melody Mayer

Delacorte Press

a nannies novel

Published by Delacorte Press
an imprint of Random House Children's Books
a division of Random House, Inc.
New York

Delacorte Press and colophon are registered trademarks
of Random House, Inc.

Visit us on the Web! www.randomhouse.com/teens
Educators and librarians, for a variety of teaching tools,
visit us at www.randomhouse.com/teachers

Library of Congress Cataloging-in-Publication Data
Mayer, Melody.
All night long : a nannies novel / by Melody Mayer. — 1st trade pbk. ed.
p. cm.
Summary: Kylie, Esme, and Lydia, nannies to the stars, rely on their friendship
as they face challenges in their work and personal lives and begin their senior
year at Bel Air High School.
ISBN: 978-0-385-73517-9 (trade pbk.)
ISBN: 978-0-385-90506-0 (Gibraltar lib. bdg.)
[1. Nannies—Fiction. 2. Interpersonal relations—Fiction. 3. Friendship—
Fiction. 4. Wealth—Fiction. 5. High schools—Fiction. 6. Schools—Fiction.
7. Beverly Hills (Calif.)—Fiction.] I. Title.
PZ7.M4619All 2008   [Fic]—dc22   2007037414

The text of this book is set in 11.25-point Berkeley Oldstyle.
Printed in the United States of America
10 9 8 7 6 5 4 3 2 1

First Edition

Once again, for my great-grandfather—
nemesis of his writers!

All Night Long

Kiley McCann

Kiley McCann stood just outside the massive doors of the Bel Air High School gym in Los Angeles—a facility that rivaled the size of, say, Madison Square Garden—and scanned the monstrous crowd for her friends. Her heart beat a tattoo in her chest and she felt her stomach cramping; she had to keep reminding herself to breathe in, breathe out, as she clenched the manila "Welcome, New Student!" packet in her sweaty hands.

Nothing was physically wrong with her. It wasn't even one of the panic attacks to which her mother was remarkably susceptible. Instead, this was an old-fashioned-if-massive case of nerves, brought on by orientation for senior year at the snootiest public school—Bel Air High—in the snootiest section of Los Angeles—Bel Air.

What, she had to ask herself, was an oh-so-average seventeen-year-old girl from La Crosse, Wisconsin, doing here?

As she unconsciously nibbled the inside of her lower lip, an annoying habit she'd had since before she could remember, and felt her Converse All Stars rooted to the tile floor, even she had to admit that the events that had brought her to this place at this moment were mind-boggling.

The audition in Milwaukee for a reality TV show, to be the nanny to the children of the rock star Platinum. The reality show getting canceled and her getting the gig anyway. Platinum getting arrested for child endangerment—could a rock star abusing drugs and alcohol in front of her children be any bigger of a cliché? And now, a chance to attend high school in California, and actually qualify for resident tuition to one of the California state universities, of which the Scripps Institution of Oceanography was by far her first choice for—

"Kiley!"

Lydia Chandler pushed her way through the masses of arriving students and threw her arms around Kiley. Suddenly, Kiley's nerves dropped to a manageable level, and she felt her heart rate return almost to normal as she looked into her blond friend's green eyes. They were shining. "Isn't this exciting?"

"Exciting" wasn't exactly the first adjective that came to Kiley's mind. "Scary." "Intimidating." Yep. Those worked. Lydia, on the other hand, never seemed to be afraid of anything. But maybe that's what growing up deep in the Amazon basin did for a girl. Kiley had met more than a few Bel Air rich girls over the summer, mostly at the tony Brentwood Hills Country Club. Lydia had told her that in Amazonia, she'd become quite accomplished with poison blow darts. Rich girls in L.A. didn't have poison darts. They had poison barbs that left you feeling just as wounded, but at least they didn't kill more than your spirit.

Like Kiley, Lydia was a nanny. Kiley knew that Lydia's route out of Amazonia and its piranha-infested waters to Beverly Hills to work for her aunt, Kat Carpenter, and Kat's lover, Anya Kuriakova, had been nearly as strange as her own. Kat was a former tennis pro turned TV sports commentator. She and Anya had had two children, Jimmy and Martina, by artificial insemination. Before she'd gone to the Amazon, Lydia had been a rich girl in Houston. She never tired of saying how the Beverly Hills life pleased her much more than life in the rain forest.

As students streamed past them into the gym, Kiley took in Lydia's naturally platinum blond hair; immense, expressive eyes; and lithe, slender body. She was clad in a very short Nanette Lepore trapeze shift in black with white polka dots, pale pink Chanel ballet flats covering her tiny feet. Kiley had been there when Lydia found the outfit at Hot Threads, the new designer "preworn" clothing store on Melrose. It was amazing. Her friend had a fantastic knack for dressing rich on a nanny's modest salary.

Damn. If I looked like Lydia, maybe I wouldn't feel so insecure.

For this all-important day, Kiley had dressed in a variation on a theme in her usual carpenter pants and a navy T-shirt. Her chestnut-reddish hair was pulled back in a ponytail. It hadn't occurred to her to do more for a school orientation. But as the people who would be her new classmates strode past her, she saw that Bel Air High girls had never met a fashion designer they couldn't acquire. Her own outfit seemed downright janitorial by comparison.

"I am so danged jazzed, I could just give birth," Lydia said. When she got excited, the Southern accent she'd acquired from living in Texas for the first several years of her life increased exponentially. That was back in the B.B., as Lydia called it—Before Banishment to a mud hut in a small hamlet of primitive Amarakaire tribesmen. How primitive? They hadn't yet developed a written language.

"It's just high school," Kiley pointed out, knowing that Lydia hadn't been in any kind of classroom other than home school since she was eight; her aunt had pulled some strings to get her into this one. Kiley, on the other hand, had spent ninth through eleventh grades at La Crosse High School, a low-slung redbrick architectural monstrosity a mile from the small house in which she'd been born and raised—with its ragged carpeting and a TV set that was broken half the time.

That her father worked for a brewery—Kiley had actually grown up in the shadow of the six-pack-painted water tower for that brewery—and her mother was a waitress at a diner did not make her stand out in any way at her old school. She knew a lot of kids who were in the same socioeconomic boat. Here at Bel Air, though, it didn't take a National Merit Scholar to figure out that her modest working-class background would make her endangered-species-level odd among her classmates.

At the computer in her guesthouse at Platinum's mansion, Kiley had read everything she could about this school to prepare for today. One of its claims to fame was that the median family income of its students was higher than those of Beverly Hills High School and Pacific Palisades High. Another distinction was that it had produced fourteen Oscar nominees over the past ten years. One more notable item was prom. She'd read through last year's online prom issue of the school newspaper—the *BAB*, as it was called, the *Bel Air Buzz*—that prom night at BAHS had cost in the low five figures. Per couple. The most sought-after prom after-party, instead of something as banal as a get-together in someone's basement or even a hotel room at the Ramada Inn, had involved a private jet to a private island in the Caribbean.

Kiley looked down resignedly at her T-shirt. Too bad there hadn't been a copy of the unofficial dress code online.

"Esme! Hey!"

Lydia put two fingers in her pouty lips and blew a shrill but very effective whistle in the direction of their other good friend—also a Hollywood nanny—Esme Castaneda. Esme, who had just walked into the gym foyer, swung her head and waved, tossing her glossy dark raven hair in the process.

Of course, two dozen other people who'd heard Lydia's whistle swung their heads as well. But Kiley noted that Lydia didn't seem to mind at all. She was too busy motioning for Esme to join them.

"Y'all, how fun is this?" Lydia threw a slim arm around Esme's shoulder. Esme didn't return the gesture. That was no shocker, since Kiley had come to know her as restrained in public and constantly wary of the overprivileged and exceedingly white world in which she operated.

Esme had been raised in the tough Echo Park neighborhood of L.A. Her parents were the undocumented Latina maid and even less documented Latino gardener for the überpowerful television producer Steven Goldhagen and his wife, Diane. When Diane returned from a trip to South America at the beginning of the summer with twin six-year-old girls she'd adopted spur-of-the-moment in Cali, Colombia (it was becoming increasingly popular for L.A.'s rich and famous to adopt kids this way), Esme had been hired to be the family nanny.

The move made sense. The twins—quickly renamed Easton and Weston—spoke no English. Diane spoke no Spanish. Esme was fluent in both languages. It was a perfect match.

"Students, please take seats in the bleachers," a melodious voice boomed over the school's sound system, loud enough to penetrate into the hall and bounce off the freshly painted walls. "If you would please take seats in the bleachers so that we can begin."

"That's our cue."

Kiley felt Lydia link her arm through hers as she led the way into the gymnasium. At first glance, it was more sports arena than gym. It featured a Jumbotron above the basketball court, the usual banners proclaiming past athletic triumphs and local advertisements, but unlike the seats at La Crosse, these bleachers were comfortably padded in the school colors of royal blue and white.

Kiley and her friends found places on the bottom row, even as kids knowingly streamed past them to jockey for the highest seats. Evidently higher was better. A trio of girls who looked as if they'd just stepped out of a *Teen Vogue* photo spread—thin, gorgeous, and perfect, clad in designer everything—brushed past them, trendily blasé and bored, regarding Kiley and her friends as if they were accident victims.

But then, the eyes swung back almost immediately to zero in on Lydia. In what must have been some kind of privileged Bel Air mind meld, the three girls all flashed flawless smiles at Kiley's friend.

Kiley might not have been familiar with the Bel Air mind-set quite yet, but she knew that smile. It said: "You exist. You're hot enough. Your two friends? Ugh!"

6

Had Esme noticed? Esme was beautiful by anyone's standards, with caramel skin and lush curves. She wore tight black trousers, red strappy heels, and a bright red tank top that showed her athletic shoulders. But Kiley realized that there were just a handful of brown-skinned kids in the entire gym.

"F them," Esme muttered.

Oh. Okay. She had noticed.

"If I could have your attention?"

A woman of indeterminate age (a description Kiley had decided was common in this world of cosmetic surgery and Botox) with streaky blunt-cut shoulder-length dark hair, clad in a taupe suit that fitted her as if it had been spray-painted on, stood on the gym floor at a microphone. She waited for her students; Kiley had learned from her Internet research that there were 640 of them. This was a reasonably big crowd to settle down, and it took quite a while for calm to prevail.

"I'm Mrs. Kwan, principal of Bel Air High, and I want to welcome all of you incoming seniors to our school. We offer a special welcome to a few new students, as well as to the student buddies who will be showing you around today."

Kiley turned and glanced up the high bleachers at the three girls who had dissed them earlier. They were about ten rows up. One was talking on her Razr, another was busily applying numerous coats of lip gloss, and the third was flirting with a cute guy next to her. Esme followed Kiley's gaze and looked too.

"Watch, they'll end up being our escorts," Esme whispered.

"I hope not."

"That's the way this shit works." Esme rolled her eyes and both girls looked back toward the gym floor, where Mrs. Kwan cleared her throat.

"I'd like to remind the entire student body to refer to me as Mrs. Kwan, not Ms. Kwan. It's a family tradition. Thank you.

"Are we ready for Evan Pace, incoming president of the senior class, to say a few words?"

The assembled students applauded politely as a tall guy in a royal blue varsity jacket strode to the mike. He had buzz-cut brown hair and a winning smile, and reminded Kiley way too much of Justin Timberlake. A few girls whistled from the back of the gym, and Evan smiled and waved confidently. Then he said all the usual welcoming things before he added a special announcement.

"So you guys who are new need to know about the kickoff senior-year event that's a tradition here at BAHS." He flashed his patented winning smile again. "It's not an official school event, so I'd better not tell you about the Up All Night party."

Around the gym, those in the know laughed, even Mrs. Kwan.

"Be sure to ask your escort about it. It's what being a senior is all about."

"Thank you, Evan," the principal said, quickly taking the microphone again. She introduced a dozen teachers, talked about various classes and clubs, then asked all the new students to take their blue and white name tags from their welcome packets and put them on.

"Your escort will find you. She or he will take you on a quick tour, introduce you to some people, answer your questions, and welcome you to our school. And of course, the door to my office is always open."

"Except when it's closed!" a voice boomed out from the top of the bleachers.

"Thank you, Chaz. Glad to see you made it through the

summer," Mrs. Kwan fired back through the laughter and titters. Meanwhile, the students took this exchange as a signal that the main affair had ended, and rose noisily. Kiley fished out her name tag and found that it was nearly the size of her hand. Well, it wouldn't be hard for her escort to find her. She'd be the one looking like a total geek.

KILEY MCCANN

LA CROSSE, WISCONSIN

Great. Why couldn't they just write on it: CHEESEHEAD LOSER.

Still, she peeled off the plastic backing and stuck the tag to her T-shirt. Lydia put on her own name tag, chortling about her hometown of Amazonia like it was a badge of honor. As for Esme, she didn't don hers at all.

"Name tag?" Kiley asked.

Esme frowned. "It says I'm from Echo Park. Everyone will decide I'm a gangbanger. If they haven't decided that already."

Kiley knew the neighborhood Esme was from very well. She'd even lived there briefly when things had gone south at Platinum's house. That was when Platinum's sister and brother-in-law had come from San Diego to be the legal guardians of the kids while Platinum was awaiting trial.

Echo Park was heavily Latino, heavily poor, and known for its gangs. It was fifteen miles and several million light-years from Bel Air.

"Maybe they'll be scared of you," Lydia pointed out. "That could work. Fear is a great motivator."

Kiley peered at Lydia to see if she was serious. Apparently, she was.

Suddenly, a gorgeous girl stepped between her and Lydia. She had stick-straight, glossy chestnut hair, huge blue eyes, and dimples. Her outfit looked like it had been designed especially for her: maroon pants so tight that they left little to the imagination, and a white silk tank top that did the same. Beside her were two friends, equally as close to perfection as anyone could be in real life. The amazing thing was, they weren't even the three girls who'd been so snotty. They were just their spiritual clones.

"Oh, fabulous, you're mine!" girl number one squealed at Lydia. "I'm Staci."

Staci's two friends introduced themselves as Amber and Zona—Amber of the dark eyes and strawberry blond razor-cut bob, Zona as blond as Lydia—with a noticeable lack of enthusiasm.

"So, you guys are friends, right?" Staci asked, brushing her hair with meticulously manicured fingers. The baby blue python purse she carried on her arm had the entwined C's logo that marked it as a Chanel bag, and was nearly as big as she was.

"How did you know?" Kiley asked.

Zona smiled. "We went through all the forms for the new seniors. You know how it asked, 'Who do you know in the senior class at BAHS?' You guys all put down each other."

"We thought it would be fun for us to take you around," Staci concluded. "Since we're best friends. Come on, follow us."

The six of them headed out of the gym and down a plush carpeted hallway that led to the center of the school. The ceiling was high, and shiny clean posters were posted on various parts of the walls. The school was shaped like the letter *X*, Staci explained, with an indoor/outdoor central area and four wings extending from there. There were three stories, and the organization was simple: administration, arts, library, and gym on the bottom; humanities on the second floor; sciences on the top.

The tour was heady. The school was gorgeous. Everything looked new and expensive and airbrushed. There was even a full-fledged oceanography laboratory that made Kiley's heart skip a beat.

"How *do* you guys know each other?" Zona asked. She was skittering along in heels so high that her legs, in skinny jeans, looked twig-like.

"It's so fabulous, we're all nannies," Lydia gushed, before Kiley could even think about stopping her. "I work for my aunt and take care of my niece and nephew, Esme works for Steven and Diane Goldhagen—you know, the producer?—and Kiley works for Platinum. Or at least she did until Platinum got arrested and went into rehab."

If it was possible for a Latina girl to pale, Kiley figured that was exactly what Esme was doing. She was a very private person, unlikely to blurt out her personal business to anyone, much less to these three girls. Lydia, on the other hand, seemed to have no verbal censor at all.

They made their way back to the central rotunda, which featured a glass-fronted office with white and blue leather couches that looked as though they had never been sat on. Next to that, in the outdoor garden area, were several round tables, each with eight seats, surrounded by a riot of exotic flowers.

Staci raked her hair off her face and squinted at Esme. "You guys are going to this school because you, like, *work* in Bel Air?"

Esme looked the girl up and down with her best Echo Park sneer. "You got a problem with that, *chica*?"

Staci was not intimidated.

"No, *chica,*" she shot back with a sneer. "I do have a problem with your outfit, because it's, like, tacky. But if that's how you want to present yourself—"

"Y'all listen up," Lydia interrupted. "We're getting off on the wrong foot." She pointed at Staci. "You dress how you want— love your outfit, by the way—and Esme will dress how she wants. Dissing a girl you don't even know—*that's* tacky."

"She's right," Zona agreed. "Besides, maybe that's how girls dress in Echo Park."

"So, what's this Up All Night thing that Evan talked about?" Kiley asked. It seemed a propitious moment to change the subject.

"Evan," Staci repeated, and sighed as if saying the name of her favorite food, then wagged a playful finger at Lydia. "He is *so* hot. Watch out. He always tries to bag the hottest new girl."

"That's such an interesting expression, 'to bag,' " Lydia mused. "Where I come from, it usually refers to a wild boar."

Staci's eyes went wide. "You really lived in the Amazon?"

"In a mud hut. Of course, before that, I was richer than Paris Hilton. Much. My parents turned into do-gooders and pretty much ruined my life."

"Oh my God, you are so cool," Zona breathed. The three girls exchanged knowing glances.

"Too true," Lydia agreed. "So are my friends." She smiled at Kiley and Esme. Kiley had no idea how Esme was taking this now. Probably not well, judging from her perma-scowl.

"Okay, so listen, you have to come with us to Up All Night," Staci gushed to Lydia. "It's an all-night party at a private beach in Malibu. Seniors only. But before we hit the beach we go party.

We'll take my dad's car and his chauffeur so we can get wasted and we won't have to drive."

Lydia nodded. "Sounds fun. As long as all six of us can go."

"Um . . ." Staci looped some glossy hair behind one ear, revealing giant diamond hoop earrings, which Kiley was pretty sure were real. "I'll have to get back to you on that. Come on, we'll show you the theater. I get the lead in all the school plays."

They headed through a portal with the helpful signage TO THE THEATER.

"What a bitch," Esme told Kiley, making no effort at all to lower her voice.

"I heard that!" Staci sang out. She was walking with Lydia in front of them.

"You want to get out of here?" Kiley whispered to Esme.

"Desperately. Hey, Lydia? Catch a ride with them!" Esme called, then tugged Kiley's arm. "Come on. Let's go."

Instead of leaving, though, they just stood and watched as Lydia and the three seniors walked together down the hall.

2

Esme Castaneda

If only the *cholos* could see her now.

In the weeks since Esme had freehanded a tattoo of a Ferris wheel on Jonathan Goldhagen's right bicep, word of her talent with a needle and ink had spread like a firestorm. She'd already been hired by Beverly Baylor, star of the indie film *Montgomery* (Jonathan was acting in that film; it was in its last days of shooting, and the wrap party was scheduled for the cowboy bar Deep South this coming Monday night), to do a tattoo of her rodeo-star lover at an hourly rate that had left Esme breathless. Her father and mother didn't earn that much money together in a *week*.

Beverly, it turned out, had a big mouth. Now all Esme had to do was sit back and enjoy the heat of her own celebrity. That was what she kept telling herself. One part of her—okay, a *big* part of her—was thrilled to have all these rich people shelling out *mucho dinero* for her tattoos. Another part of her wanted to tell them all to go to hell.

She knew she was exotic—a girl from Echo Park who didn't use stencils when she went to work with her needle and ink. The whole exotic thing was amusing. She'd recently heard that Los Angeles had a larger Latino population than white population. Not that you'd know it from the circles in which people like Jonathan and Beverly operated, where, generally speaking, the only Latinos they came in contact with were wearing a uniform or carrying hedge shears.

It was the day after the orientation, which had been so disheartening. Well, what the hell. It was just school. She'd endured it for years in Echo Park, she could endure it for one year at Bel Air High. At least most of the students would show up for class, she figured. Today, Esme was at the Brentwood Hills Country Club, wearing a red polka-dot bikini with side ties that she'd found in a seventy-five-percent-off bin at a boutique on Melrose because the stitching was ragged under the bust. Esme had easily hidden the frayed stitching with some red thread and her father's hot glue gun.

Her legs were freshly shaved and she brushed her fingers over her dark skin. She rolled onto her back and bent one knee, relaxing on a chaise under the warm afternoon sun. She'd met up at the club with Lydia so that they could soak up some rays by the adult pool while Martina, Easton, and Weston were at the main clubhouse for makeovers.

It was hard for Esme to believe that makeovers for children could be part of the country club's children's programming. When she was a girl, makeovers meant getting into her mother's limited supplies of cosmetics and going to town with one of her lipsticks. But that absurd world was now where she lived, where professional makeup artists made house calls and carried around briefcases full of dollars, euros, and dinars, depending on what currency their clients wanted to use. Absurd. Like those girls at the orientation session for school. They were quintessentially absurd. Esme didn't want to care that they'd dissed her and Kiley. But she did care. More than she wanted to admit.

She and Lydia had ordered lunch from the luxurious clubhouse restaurant—lobster salad, pâté with fresh-baked French bread, a huge fruit salad, and two bottles of Perrier. Lydia kept trying to talk to Esme about her strategy for winning back her boyfriend, Billy, who had recently dumped her—not without reason, Esme thought. But the conversation sputtered because tattoo customers—or at least, potential tattoo customers—kept interrupting.

"Pardon me, miss, but is your name Esme?"

A fortyish woman with her hair tucked under a straw hat with a massive brim, oversized white sunglasses, and a body overflowing from a black Gottex bikini peered down at her. An impatient foot in a white Anne Klein matte-and-metallic-leather slide tapped next to her chair.

Before Esme could respond, Lydia sat up on her chaise lounge. She was in Chanel sunglasses and a white crocheted string bikini, which set off her golden tan and pale hair. Esme knew that the bathing suit, as was true of so much of Lydia's wardrobe, had formerly belonged to her aunt Kat. There was only so far one could go on a nanny's salary.

"That depends on who you're asking for," Lydia said. "Would that be Esme Castaneda, nanny extraordinaire? Or Esme Castaneda, tattoo artist to the stars?"

The woman smiled, displaying Chiclet-white teeth. "I suppose that my Esme is the latter. I'm Jacqueline Grace, you may have heard of me?"

Esme mulled the name over and came up with zip. Why did everyone in Hollywood think that everyone who wasn't connected to Hollywood should instantly recognize them?

She looked at Lydia, who shrugged, meaning she couldn't place her, either.

Jacqueline sighed. "We documentary producers get no respect. I was nominated for an Oscar last year. The one about the wheelchair athletes? That was mine."

"Congrats on the nomination," Lydia offered. "Where I come from, we didn't get movies, much less documentaries."

"Goodness!" Jacqueline exclaimed.

Lydia nodded solemnly. "Entertainment was watching monkeys mate. Which, if you've never seen it, can be very—"

"What can I do for you?" Esme interrupted.

Jacqueline turned and pointed to the back of her long, slender neck. "Ever do a tattoo here?"

Esme nodded. "Can't say I have. But it's doable. Skin is skin."

"I'm here for meetings and going back to New York on Monday, so I wondered if on Sunday you could come by the Beverly Hills Hotel and do me."

"She's totally straight, but she appreciates the offer," Lydia told her without blinking.

Jacqueline laughed. "You're quick, I like that. If I do something on young women in Bel Air, you'll have to be in it. Anyway, I'd like a dove there. That's my favorite bird. A white dove. Outlined maybe in magenta, or black. Eight-fifty flat fee sound good? I know it's short notice. But I have my fortieth birthday party a week from tonight at Jubilee in Manhattan, and I want to wow my friends. I hear you're an artist, Esme."

Esme was about to accede when Lydia cut in. "Sorry, but it's just not possible. Esme's schedule is completely booked for at least four weeks." She blithely squirted a generous dose of SPF 15 on her forearms and worked it in.

Esme shot Lydia a look that she hoped said *Shut the hell up.*

Jacqueline cleared her throat. "If money is the issue, I could pay double that, or even—"

"Double is fine. I'll move some things, clear my schedule, it's a deal," Esme said quickly, removing her sunglasses and squinting at the woman in the bright overhead sunlight.

"Perfect! Here's my card. I'll be working in my bungalow all day on Sunday. Just call in the morning and tell me when you're coming." Jacqueline extracted a business card from the oversized white leather bag on her arm and pressed it into Esme's outstretched hand.

"Cash," Lydia told her. "Esme takes cash only. No credit cards. No check."

That wasn't exactly true. She'd taken checks on more than one occasion. But cash would be good, if Jacqueline—

"Of course. Is there anything else?"

"How'd you get my name?" Esme wondered aloud.

"Beverly Baylor. She's a friend of my husband's." Making the motion of holding a phone by her ear as a signal for Esme to call her, Jacqueline flounced happily away toward the far end of the crowded pool deck.

When she was out of earshot, Lydia plucked the business card from Esme's hand. "Are you crazy? You could have asked for triple. She was ready to pay it. You just released the catch of the day."

"She's already paying too much," Esme protested.

Lydia gave a long-suffering sigh. "You really should hire me as your business manager. I could make you a fortune."

Esme was not about to take Lydia up on that offer. Not long after they'd met, Lydia had come up with a brilliant can't-miss scheme to start a nanny placement business. That had turned out to be far more trouble than it was worth, and Lydia hadn't even talked about it in a long time. Of the three friends, Esme was making by far the most money. Tattoo artistry was definitely not a team sport. "I don't need anyone. In fact, before we were so rudely interrupted, we were talking about how much *you* need *me*."

Lydia sighed. "It's killing me, but it's true. Look around."

"Why?"

"Just do it."

Esme did. Brentwood Hills was the most exclusive country club in Los Angeles—it regularly turned down members of Riviera—and the adult pool deck was a paparazzo's dream . . . as if any photographer could hope to gain admission. Surrounding the adult pool (there was a separate pool for the kids) were wicker chaise lounges and hefty sun umbrellas at discreet intervals around the white pool deck. Stretched out on those lounges was a decent cross section of Hollywood's rich and famous. Esme spotted two of the younger stars of *Heroes* and another from *The Young and the Restless,* while Tom Hanks and his wife were huddled with Martin Scorsese twenty or thirty feet away. Directly across the pool from them was a cluster of guys who had to be male models. The incredibly hot bodies and shaved chests were a dead giveaway.

"What do you see?" Lydia demanded.

"Same thing you see. Overprivileged buffdom."

"Yes, but none of the buffs are Billy Martin."

Esme squinted at her friend. Lydia wanted Esme to do her a favor, which had to do with Lydia winning back her boyfriend.

"Maybe I should charge you for what you want me to do," she teased.

"You'll do it because you love me," Lydia said sweetly. "And because you don't want me to suffer for one teeny tiny momentary lapse of judgment. Here. Taste the lobster. It's to die for."

Lydia forked a buttery chunk of lobster and popped it into Esme's mouth. It was delicious, melting in her mouth and sliding down her throat, just as advertised. The crustacean was awesome. What Lydia was asking her to do wasn't.

The week before, Lydia had made a horrendous mistake. She'd cheated on Billy. Well, it wasn't exactly cheating, because Billy and Lydia hadn't had sex yet. Trust Lydia, who'd been dying to find the perfect boy and jettison her virginity, to fall for the only guy in Southern California who wanted a Real Relationship before sex. Lydia said many times that if the Ama tribesmen in the Amazon had been more attractive—over five feet tall, say, or with teeth that lasted past age thirty—she might well have lost said virginity in a mud hut.

Instead, Lydia had done something supremely stupid: she'd gotten drunk and hooked up with a golf pro here at the club. His name was Luis. He was a college student at nearby Pepperdine. Then, to make matters worse, Luis would not accept the fact that Lydia wasn't interested in a relationship with him. He was so pissed off that he'd tracked Lydia down and returned to her the T-shirt she had forgotten at his bungalow. That wouldn't have been so bad, except that Lydia had been with Billy at the time. Hello, Hanes. Bye-bye, Billy.

Which led to the favor Lydia was now requesting. She wanted Esme to assure Billy that Lydia had never cheated on him. That Luis was just pissed at Lydia because she'd shot him down, and this was merely his petty act of revenge.

"You could see him tonight," Lydia coaxed. "I know where he'll be."

"Where?" Esme took a long swallow of Perrier.

"He and his friend X are going to the Derby in Los Feliz. Maybe you could by-mistake-on-purpose run into them."

Esme noted the desperate look on Lydia's face, though Lydia never seemed to feel desperate about anything.

"Maybe," Esme agreed.

Impulsively, Lydia reached across the space between them and hugged Esme hard. "Thanks. You have no idea how much this means to me."

"Actually, I do. But you don't have to owe me one." She stood, stretching her sun-warmed limbs, and reached a hand down to her friend. "Come on. Let's walk to the clubhouse and see what the kids look like made over."

Lydia laughed. "Better than we do, I'm sure."

On a normal day, the kids' play area in the main clubhouse was heaven on earth for anyone under the age of twelve. Every game and toy in the universe; multiple wall-mounted plasma TVs with Xboxes, PS-whatevers, and Wiis up the wazoo; a soft, matted floor for roughhousing; and fridges and freezers full of snacks and drinks. Sometimes, no matter how much fun was planned for the kids on the rest of the club's expansive grounds, it was hard to get the children out of the playroom, even though most of them had playrooms of their own at their respective mansions and estates.

21

Today, though, the play area had been transformed. All the boys had been bused off to Will Rogers State Park on the way to Malibu for a surfing/boogie board experience. That left all the girls in the Nanny and Me program—upward of twenty or twenty-five girls—in the hands of a small army of stylists, makeup artists, haircutters, and their many assistants, equipped with the most expensive products and tools straight off the runway. It cost a small fortune, but the clientele of the club could afford it.

When Esme and Lydia arrived, they saw many of the other nannies they knew standing in a cluster at the west end of the room, since a large red curtain had been drawn dividing the room in half. Though they didn't do a lot of socializing with these nannies away from the club, they said hello to Claudette from Cameroon, Judith from Quebec City, Marielle from France, Sophie from Montreal, and Françoise from Belgium. Esme realized there was a real prejudice at the club toward francophone nannies.

Suddenly, rock music began to pound, and the head of the Nanny and Me program, an aggressively enthusiastic African American woman named Sandra with beautifully relaxed hair and bright red lipstick, stepped out onto the mat. "Welcome, nannies and parents! To the first annual Nanny and Me makeover day!"

The nannies applauded politely. Esme checked the crowd—no mothers in sight. Typical. Just like Diane Goldhagen, the woman for whom she worked, most of the country club mothers were content to let their nannies drive their kids to the club while they shopped, primped, or did volunteer work.

"We've brought in makeup artists from Warner Brothers, stylists from Fred Segal, and the entire haircutting crew from Alexander Paisan in Beverly Hills. Just wait till you see the little darlings. Modeling could just be in their futures!" Sandra swept a well-toned arm outward without a hint of tricep waddle. "Pull back the curtain! Show this crowd their made-over kids!"

The red curtain opened with a flourish, revealing an assortment of girls ranging from the Goldhagen twins at age six to a couple of girls Françoise took care of who were allegedly fourteen but could easily have passed for nineteen (despite a maturity level somewhere closer to ten). In the middle of the pack was ten-year-old Martina. Martina was one of those unfortunate girls who'd reached puberty before her time and tried to hide her conspicuous breasts under baggy, inconspicuous clothing.

Esme spotted Easton and Weston Goldhagen immediately, but she had to do a double take to be sure it was them. At the start of the morning, they'd had long, lush hair. Now, Easton had a trendy razor-cut bob, and Weston's hair had been crimped, with red and gold streaks added on the sides.

"Holy shit. What will Diane say about their hair?" Esme was incredulous.

But Lydia wasn't even paying attention. "Get a load of my niece. They've turned Martina into a babe."

Lydia pointed, and Esme literally gasped. Martina's normally limp brown hair, which she habitually shook over her dark eyes so that she could hide from the world, had been moussed into tousled waves. Her eyebrows had obviously been plucked; she wore a touch of mascara and clear lip gloss. Gone were the baggy clothes in which she'd begun the day, replaced by a cute purple-polka-dotted peasant shirt over white capri leggings with lace bottoms. In these new clothes, it was clear that formerly pudgy Martina had lost a lot of weight on her summer exercise program. With her new look, and clothes that didn't approximate a circus tent, it was easy to see the results.

Lydia cupped her hands. "Martina, you cutie! Woo-hoo! C'mere and gimme a hug!"

Martina broke into a wide grin and ran toward Lydia behind the velvet rope. Esme took that as her cue to duck under the barrier and talk to the twins, who were already halfway toward her when Esme heard a lilting voice with a Jamaican accent call to them from the other side of the room.

"Easton! Weston! Come to Tarshea and your mother!"

The kids instantly did a ninety-degree turn, forgetting about Esme and bolting toward their mother. Diane Goldhagen was blond, thin, and beautiful, and must have come straight from the gym, since she wore a jet-black Adidas warm-up suit. Even in sweats, she looked as if she'd stepped out of an advertisement for the Southern California good life.

That was fine. But who was with Diane wasn't so fine. Esme narrowed her eyes in disgust.

When the Goldhagen family had taken a vacation to Jamaica, they'd brought Esme along. On that trip, they'd met a young Jamaican woman named Tarshea, who'd spoken longingly of coming to America. The Goldhagens, after they'd returned to Los Angeles, had hastily arranged a visa for Tarshea, with the idea that they could find her a nanny job here. That was good. Unfortunately, Diane had taken a liking to Tarshea. Now the girl was sort of a co-nanny with Esme. That was bad. Esme liked Tarshea in theory. In practice, it felt as if the girl was taking over her life. She'd even showed more than a little interest in Esme's new boyfriend, who happened to be the Goldhagens' son, Jonathan.

"¡Mira a Tarshea!" Weston called over her shoulder.

"I'm looking," Esme replied.

Tarshea had always been a pretty girl, with her long, graceful neck, slender body, and huge dark eyes. She'd braided her frizzy hair because, as she'd explained to Esme, she didn't know what else to do with it. Now, Tarshea's hair fell straight and glossy to her shoulders like a crown. Her eyes had been enhanced with subtle smoky makeup, her lips burnished copper with some sort of product to make them even more pouty. She wore a very short orange Chloé slip dress that Esme had gawked at in a boutique window on Third Street. The dress showcased her long, slender legs. On her feet were chic brown suede ballet flats with crisscross ties around the ankles.

Either Tarshea had gotten a makeover here at the club, or she'd gone with Diane for one at another location.

Jeez. It was one thing for Tarshea to be gorgeous; Esme wouldn't begrudge the girl, who came from such terrible poverty in Jamaica, a chance to shine. It was the fact that Diane was smiling at Tarshea as if she was her own long-lost daughter, and the twins were tugging on her hands. The thought of Jonathan seeing Tarshea looking like this put Esme over the top.

Esme had ample reason to suspect that Tarshea wanted her life. She borrowed her clothes all the time without asking, and had tried to horn in on her friends more than once. In the nicest possible way, of course. But it was more than that. From the way she'd seen Tarshea act around Jonathan, she suspected that Tarshea didn't just want her life. She wanted her boyfriend, too.

3

Lydia Chandler

As Lydia stepped into the crowded Silverbird Lounge in Los Feliz, she thought it was a very, very good sign that Billy had asked to meet her at this particular club. This nightspot—famous for the mechanical silver birds that, by some feat of engineering, flew around the club high over the patrons' heads every fifteen minutes—was the place where she and Billy had first met.

She remembered that night well. It hadn't been all that long after she had met Kiley and Esme, and she'd decided to go out clubbing on her own. X, her aunt's driver, had dropped her there, then headed off to a gay club in West Hollywood. She'd found a place at the bar and immediately discovered the joy and fun of having random men offer to buy her cocktails. Almost immediately, she'd taken a liking to something called a California Condor—rum, Red Bull, Kahlua, and milk, topped by a splash of eggnog.

X had come back to pick her up and had brought Billy with him. For sure, Lydia had decided, Billy was gay. First, he was close friends with X, who was unequivocally gay and had better fashion sense than nearly anyone she had met. Second, he had the chiseled good looks of the denizens of West Hollywood, for whom skin, face, and body were high priorities. Only it turned out that by some miracle Billy Martin wasn't gay. That changed everything. And the fact that he'd been raised by parents in the Foreign Service, which meant he shared some of Lydia's experience of being a stranger in a strange land, had brought them even closer.

"Hey, want to dance when the music starts?"

Lydia wasn't even halfway to the bar when the first guy hit on her. He was in his twenties, with tattoos of dragons covering both arms, and the tight black pants/tight black shirt combination of a metal rocker.

"Can't, meeting my *girl*friend," she told him.

"I remember this town before lesbian chic," the rocker lamented.

"Get a boyfriend. Excuse me, I'm getting a drink."

"Make that two drinks."

Lydia turned. It was Billy. He was wearing black cowboy boots that made him even taller than his six foot two inches, and his light brown hair was short and spiky. He wore a simple light blue dress shirt with the sleeves rolled up, and black boot-cut jeans that highlighted his toned thighs. Next to him, in a white Stella McCartney slip dress short enough to make Sienna Miller's shortest seem floor-length, she felt like a shrimp. A shrimp, however, that was in very good handsome company.

"Hey," she said softly.

"Hey, yourself."

"Wait—I thought you were gay!" the tattooed rocker protested to her.

"One look at this guy and I went bi. Can you blame me?"

With a wink at the rocker guy, she took Billy's arm and followed him past the bar and into the quieter back room. There, the bird theme continued, with paintings of parrots and other exotica on the walls, and feathered couches and loves seats. There was soft jazz playing in the background, instead of the raucous rock out front, and waiters with brightly colored outfits served multicolored drinks.

Billy laughed as they headed for an unoccupied seat toward the rear covered in pink flamingo feathers.

"What's so funny?" Lydia asked.

"That music. It's Charlie Parker. His nickname was Bird," Billy explained.

They sat in the love seat, and a waitress in black and yellow took their order for two California Condors. Then Billy looked at her with his soulful eyes. "I owe you an apology."

The waitress had left a couple of bottles of Poland Spring water on the low table in front of them—a nice touch, Lydia thought, in a city where tap water was notoriously disgusting. She opened one and drank as Billy pressed on.

"Your friend Esme talked to me last night. At the Derby."

"She did?" Lydia feigned ignorance.

"Come on. You had to know she did. How else would she have known where to find me?"

"I might have mentioned that," Lydia agreed. "But I'd never ask her to talk to you."

"Well, she did anyway," Billy explained. "Good friend."

The lights in the back room dimmed slightly, and the music

shifted to an exotic solo piano. "Chick Corea," Billy pronounced as the waitress set their Condors down. They were served in large, opaque, egg-shaped glasses.

"Is there anything you don't know about?" Lydia joked.

Billy's face got serious. "I don't know why I overreacted about you and the golf pro," he admitted. "How's that for starters?"

Lydia smiled. "Pretty danged good."

"I assumed the worst," Billy continued, "when what's-his-name—Luis?—came to the hotel when we were there. I don't know. There was just something about that smug asshole."

"He is an asshole." Lydia wiped the condensation off the side of her drink.

"Just assure me of one thing."

"Anything."

He looked at her closely. "You never did the guy. Right?"

Lydia raised her right hand the way she'd seen people do in movies. "Billy Martin, I wouldn't let that guy touch me with a ten-foot nine-iron."

He kept his eyes on her for a moment, then picked up his drink and cradled it thoughtfully. "I talked to him this morning. Face to face."

Uh-oh. This was bad. Very, very bad.

"You went to see him?" Lydia asked. "When?"

"This morning. At the club."

She puffed some air out of her lips in what she hoped was controlled nonchalance. "What did Prince Charming have to say?"

"A crock of shit about your alleged night together."

Lydia looked up at him. "As long as you know it was a crock."

"The guy's a dick. If you were going to cheat on me, I know it wouldn't be with a lowlife like him."

Ouch. "I wouldn't cheat on you at all," Lydia insisted. She scooched up against Billy's broad shoulder. Hearing all this made her feel terrible. There was nothing she could do to turn back the clock, but at least she'd learned from her mistake. She could only imagine what Luis had told Billy. The worst part was that Luis hadn't had to make much up. She couldn't help it— she wondered whether Luis had said anything about it being her very first time.

"I told the schmuck to stay the hell away from you," Billy reported. "And that's all I want to say about him for the rest of my life."

"You and me both."

"You let me know if he gives you any grief. I think he got my message."

The music picked up, and a few couples rose from their couches or love seats to dance. Lydia leaned in toward Billy and indicated the dancing couples. "Let's finish our drinks and go do what they're doing."

His answer was to drain his Condor, motion to the waitress for two more, and lead Lydia to the dance floor. Somehow, being in his arms, swaying to the music, was a lot easier than talking. She gave herself over to the smooth rhythms and let the music take her away to someplace where no one had even heard of an assistant golf pro named Luis.

"Good morning."

Kat's greeting was understated as Lydia slipped into the brightly lit kitchen the next morning at eight-thirty. The large windows reflected sunlight and another clear blue California day, and Lydia's head pulsed slightly. She felt mildly hungover—she and Billy had stayed out until the club closed, polishing off several more California Condors in the interim. Lydia had half hoped that Billy would take her back to his place in Venice—or at least offer to take her back—but it wasn't meant to be. She had to work this afternoon, and he was supposed to go to LAX to meet his parents, who were coming in from Washington, D.C., on a red-eye. They'd made plans to talk to each other on Sunday night and try to get together on Tuesday, and that was it. Lydia did mention that her cousin Jimmy was absolutely dying to go to a Dodgers game, and Billy had responded with enthusiasm. They were at home on Tuesday afternoon. Maybe he could take Jimmy to the game, and then he and Lydia could go out Tuesday night? Lydia thought that was a wonderful plan.

"Morning," Lydia replied. "Where is everyone?"

Kat, who was dressed in a pair of men's blue-and-white-striped gym shorts and a T-shirt from the 1994 championships at Wimbledon—where she'd reached round sixteen in singles and the quarterfinals in mixed doubles—made a face. "It's just me. Martina and Jimmy spent the night with some friends from the club. And Anya? Anya's at the club. Playing golf. Anya's always playing golf. You want coffee?"

"I'd love coffee."

"I made some with these beans from Kenya. They're the best." Kat indicated a smooth white carafe on the stone counter. Lydia poured some into the brown earthenware cup. She took it black. Back in Amazonia, the notion of milk in coffee meant a need for reliable refrigerators—there were none—or milk that came directly from the goats. However, there were plenty of coffee beans, some of which were harvested right there in the jungle.

"Thanks." Lydia sat down at the glass kitchen table. It was covered with fingerprints from the kids, and Anya was forever spraying Windex on it and wiping, despite the fact that she and Kat had more help than most five-star hotels.

"You know, I honestly can't remember the last time I was here at the house by myself," Kat observed. "That's what having kids does to you."

Lydia inhaled the delicious coffee aroma. "I used to spend a lot of time alone in the rain forest. Hunting, fishing, whatever. When no one speaks your language except your mom and dad, you get really interested in your own company."

Kat smiled. "Have you heard from your parents?"

"Nope." Lydia shook her head. "And I don't expect to, either. Not until they go upriver to Manaus." Manaus, in Brazil, was the closest town to where Lydia had lived in the jungle. "Close" being a relative term, of course. It was a brutal hundred miles away via the piranha-infested rugged waters of Rio Negro.

"Well, if you do, remind them that I'll be in New York starting next week. For the U.S. Open. You think you can hold the fort down here with Anya?"

"Sure, why not?"

Actually, there were a number of reasons why not. That Lydia suspected supposedly gay Anya was cheating on Kat with Kiley's definitely male boss—of all people!—was only one of them. That Anya had the charm of a drill instructor in the Russian army was another.

Kat bit into one of the freshly baked croissants she took from a wicker basket on the table and shook her head ruefully. "I remember—this was before we had the kids—Sunday morning was our time. For Anya and me, I mean. We'd stay in bed until noon. Hell, sometimes we'd stay in bed until dinner. Now, it's like all she wants to do is play golf. This morning, we had a chance for one of those before-the-kids mornings. The alarm rang at seven—she was out the door at seven-thirty. Eight o'clock tee time, she claimed."

Lydia was so tempted to just spill it all to her aunt. Tell her what she knew about Anya, and how Anya was cheating on her. But what did she know, really? That she caught Anya making a phone-sex call? Kat already knew that. That Anya had a copy of the *Kama Sutra* hidden in her closet? Fine, maybe she liked erotica. Maybe the idea of being with a guy turned her on. Maybe she and Kat used it, in some way that Lydia couldn't imagine. Maybe that was all it was, though. Fantasy.

You know in your gut, she told herself. *You know.*

Sure. But what if you're wrong? You could destroy everything for your aunt. And for the kids.

"Maybe you need to take up golf, too," Lydia suggested.

Kat finished her coffee and wiped her mouth with a white silk napkin. "Golf? A horrid way to spend four or five hours. If I want to take a walk in a park, I'll take a walk in a park. Thank you, but I'll stick to tennis. Excuse me. I think I'm going to go swim some laps."

Without another word, Kat padded out of the kitchen, leaving Lydia alone. It was just as well. Lydia needed to think. She refilled her coffee cup and took it out through the sliding glass doors onto the redwood deck that adjoined the kitchen. There was a hole in the floor of the deck large enough for the trunk of a palm tree that soared from the ground up through the deck toward the sky. From here, Lydia could watch as Kat walked out to the pool, stripped off her top and shorts, and then dove into the crystal water wearing just her black underwear. With strong, determined strokes, she cut through the water with her tennis player's arms.

Lydia felt awful for her. But she didn't have proof. And without actual proof, she wasn't ready to have the conversation with Kat that would surely result in the destruction of her relationship, and her children losing a parent. Lydia didn't care that Kat had asked to hear about any and all suspicious activity that she saw. Proof was required.

But . . . that didn't mean she had to do nothing. Right then and there, she decided that she'd have a serious talk with Anya. Tell her what she knew and what she'd seen. And tell Anya that she'd better get her shit together. Lydia knew Anya's drill. She'd get mad, she'd bluster, she'd bullshit. But Lydia didn't care. As she watched her mother's sister take out her aggression in the swimming pool, she knew that would be the right thing to do.

4

Before she even saw the crowd, Kiley could hear the buzz in the air. She walked across the hot pavement holding Serenity by one hand and Sid by the other. Platinum's sister Susan and her ramrod-straight husband, known to one and all as the colonel, walked four paces ahead of them. Slouching along behind them was Bruce, Platinum's fourteen-year-old son, clad in a suit jacket over a "Free Platinum" T-shirt, which he was now flashing at the crowd held back by police barricades.

It wasn't a crowd, Kiley decided. It was a mob. One part paparazzi, two parts family-values activists, and ten parts fans obsessed as only fans in Los Angeles could be. It had gathered in front of the gleaming white stone Beverly Hills courthouse to witness the start of Platinum's trial for the reckless endangerment of her kids. The same kids who'd been exposed to and endangered by her flagrant drug use. The same kids Kiley McCann tended to daily. The same kids whose hands she was holding at that very moment.

Then there were the drug charges. The police had found marijuana in plain sight in Platinum's living room. But drug charges were a dime a dozen in Los Angeles. It was the child endangerment that was captivating the gossip columnists and television pundits.

Sid made himself belch as loudly as possible, over and over.

"Stop it, Sid, you suck!" Serenity screamed.

"Nuh-uh, *you* suck!" Sid yelled back.

Both of them had a tendency to use bad language when they got upset or anxious.

"It's going to be okay, you guys," Kiley assured them, even as the paparazzi and fans recognized the kids and began snapping their pictures.

Serenity stopped to pose, as if on the red carpet at a movie premiere. This morning she'd insisted on getting up at five a.m. It meant Kiley had to get up, too, to get ready to go to the trial. Serenity had tried on outfit after outfit, all of them better suited for an MTV music video than for a girl about to start the third grade. Kiley knew that the colonel—Serenity's uncle by marriage—would make the little girl take off said outfit as soon as he saw it. She warned Serenity that this was so. But somewhere in the world of kid logic, Serenity thought she'd be able to get away with it anyway.

When the little girl came down for breakfast in the bright green halter top and low-slung plaid boyfriend pants that bared her navel and a good two inches of pale little-girl flesh below it, sure enough, the colonel had ordered her to turn around and march right back upstairs. She now sported a pair of khaki pants and a pale blue short-sleeved polo.

Now, though, as Serenity posed, Kiley realized that some-where along the way, the little girl had put on cherry red lip gloss, mascara, and blush. Up ahead, the colonel and Susan were heading into the security clearance area in front of the courthouse. He turned, saw that Kiley and the kids had stopped and that Bruce was actually signing autographs, and motioned them forward impatiently.

"Free my mom! Free my mom!" Sid began to chant.

Kiley could feel the colonel's glower from fifty paces away. She really, really disliked the man. According to Lydia, the colonel was cheating on his wife with Lydia's nonhetero boss, Anya Kuriakova. Lydia claimed to have caught them red-handed on the club golf course, with his marine-saluting palm on Anya's tush. Kiley liked Susan, Platinum's sister. The idea that her asshole of a husband was cheating on her—

"Free Platinum now! Free Platinum now!" the crowd chanted in response to Sid, who was pumping his fist in the air.

Kiley tugged the kids forward. "Come on, we have to go." The kids might feel at home in this circus, but Kiley's churning stomach told her she had a long way to go.

"Bruce, is it true you did drugs with your mom?"

"Sid! Serenity! This way!"

"*Entertainment Tonight*—if I could just talk with you a moment!"

Kiley tried to tune out all the voices coming at them and urged the kids forward.

"Kiley! Hey, Kiley!"

She recognized that voice, and turned to try to locate it in the crowd. Tom Chappelle, the six-foot blond model who by some fluke of nature Kiley was dating, was muscling his way toward her. In an old blue tennis shirt and faded jeans, he looked better than anyone else looked in a tux.

"Tom!" she shouted back, and the reporters pressed closer to her.

"Are you and Kiley a couple? Did you see kids doing drugs at Platinum's house?" one reporter shouted.

"No comment," Tom called over his shoulder. "Hey." He hugged Kiley. All around them, people snapped their embrace with cameras and cell phones. Tom, after all, was famous. Kiley felt utterly, hopelessly self-conscious.

"What are you doing here?" Kiley asked him.

"Same as everybody. I'm here to see Platinum," Tom teased.

Kiley whapped him on the shoulder.

"I came for you, Miss McCann." He gave her a dazzling smile. "But if you want me to head back into that teeming crowd—"

"God, no!" Kiley exclaimed. "Thanks for coming. It means a lot to me."

"McCann!" the colonel boomed, hands cupped to his mouth. "Front and center, double-time!"

"That guy so rubs me the wrong way," Tom muttered.

Kiley's reply was lost in the roar of the crowd, which began chanting Platinum's name. Kiley turned. The rock star had just emerged from her silver stretch limo with a burly bodyguard on each side, and they, the sheriffs, and her trio of attorneys began to move toward the courthouse steps.

"Mom!" Serenity cried. "Wow. Why is she dressed so weird?"

It occurred to Kiley that by "weird," Serenity meant "normal." Kiley could not remember Platinum looking more businesslike. In a gray skirt suit and wide Chanel sunglasses, she looked about as serious and determined as her lead lawyer, Richie Singleton. Richie was straight out of central casting. African American, with a trim mustache, wearing an immaculate Ralph Lauren suit with a yellow power tie, he was all business.

"Mom!" Sid yelled, jumping up and down and waving his arms.

Platinum spotted her children pushing through the crowd toward her. Richie gave his lawyerly nod of blessing, and Platinum scooped up Sid in one suited arm and Serenity in the other while Bruce hugged the three from the side. If it wasn't for Kiley's knowledge of Platinum's underappreciated acting prowess, she would swear that the rock star's joyous tears came from the heart and not from the opportunity for good press.

Then Platinum motioned to Kiley, blinking teary false lashes. "Come on in here! You're part of the family, too!" Sid and Serenity opened their arms to welcome Kiley as the photographers did their thing.

Kiley obliged, even though she felt absolutely ridiculous.

Someone pushed a microphone into Platinum's face. She turned to address the throng. "I just want the members of the media and the whole city of Los Angeles to know that I'm innocent. I will be acquitted of all the charges. And I will get my kids back. Now, thank you for coming out. It means the world to me."

Cheers erupted among nine-tenths of the crowd. A few family-values naysayers catcalled at the fringes, but they were quickly drowned out by the cheers.

"My lawyers and I will fight tooth and nail to get this lamebrain bull"—Richie shook his head with wide eyes at hearing the red flag—"crud overturned."

More cheering. Kiley knew from experience that Platinum was not one to curb her language, but if ever there was a time for it, it was now. Near the back, she noticed a group of people holding a banner with the words PLATINUM 4EVA in neat red lettering. Then it became impossible to hear or talk, because a news helicopter started circling overhead.

"We need to go in now," Platinum's lawyer insisted, and the group headed for the courthouse steps, where the colonel and Susan had long been waiting. Kiley and Tom brought up the rear.

"Ms. McCann, a moment?" A handsome middle-aged man in an impeccable charcoal Armani suit and wingtip shoes approached Kiley.

"Spencer Lacroix," he said, introducing himself. Kiley saw Platinum and the kids disappear inside with her entourage.

Tom put a protective arm around Kiley. "We need to go in, Kiley—"

"I only need a moment, Mr. Chappelle," the older man insisted. "I loved your work in *The Ten,* by the way."

The Ten was a blockbuster movie in which Tom had had a small role.

Once Tom had moved away, Mr. Lacroix wasted no time in pulling a small envelope from his breast pocket and offering it to Kiley. "There's five hundred dollars in there. Buy something nice to wear to court tomorrow."

Kiley furrowed her brow and tried to hand back the envelope. "I don't know who you are or what you want, but I don't want your money."

"It's a gift. It would be rude to refuse a gift, wouldn't it?" Mr. Lacroix said smugly before registering Kiley's distrust. "I'm editor in chief of the *Universe*? The most-read celebrity magazine in the entire world?"

Kiley knew the *Universe*. It was right up there with the *Star* and *People,* though it had a reputation for being more of a scandal sheet.

"I see from the look on your face you know my magazine," Mr. Lacroix continued. "And here's what I know. You're Platinum's nanny from Wisconsin, your mom's name is Jeanne, and you're starting at Bel Air High in the fall. I also know that if anybody could use a big increase in their bottom line, it's you."

Kiley's stomach tightened. "What do you want?" She felt Tom's arm tighten around her shoulders.

The editor leaned closer. "If you want two hundred more of those envelopes with your name on 'em, all you have to do is sit down with us for a nice easy talk on Platinum. I'm talking a hundred thousand dollars."

But wait. That couldn't be right. She had to double-check. "Did you just say—"

"Six figures starting with a one," he confirmed. "All you have to do is tell us about Platinum. The inside scoop the outside world wants to know."

Kiley couldn't imagine betraying Platinum. Even worse would be betraying the kids, who trusted her completely. She thrust the envelope back at Spencer Lacroix.

"I'm sorry. I'm not the right person for this. You'll have to get someone else."

As if Kiley was threatening him, Lacroix backed away with his hands up.

"Whoa, Kiley. Not so fast. Look, I'll let you in on a little secret. The *Universe* is going to run the story anyway. We know all about the household, the drugs, the neglect. As far as your boss is concerned, the damage is already done. Platinum is bound for jail, these kids are going to be under the protection of the state, and the only thing you can do is think about your own future. All we want is a few quotes. You might as well get a little recompense for your trouble." He took two more steps back. "Spencer Lacroix. I'll find you."

Then he turned on his heel and left as smoothly as he had appeared.

Kiley hustled through the courthouse doors and took the elevator to the courtroom. There was a mob scene right outside the courtroom too, but down the hall a little bit, Kiley noticed Platinum's lead attorney pacing. His face lit up when he saw her. "There you are! Thought you might have abandoned ship. But I should have known, you got that McCann-do attitude."

Singleton adjusted his glasses. "Ms. McCann, I tried to contact you sooner about this, but I'll have to tell you now. I'm going to need you to testify. It won't be until later this week, but it's crucially important. Please tell me I can count on you."

Well, this wasn't unexpected. But if she was going to testify in a court of law, she would do it on her own terms. "Yes. I'll testify. But only if I can tell the truth."

A wide smile spread across Singleton's lips as he opened the mahogany door. "That's all I ask. Now hurry inside, you two, before you miss the big entrance."

The courtroom was the biggest in the building. Rows of seating for a hundred spectators, the judge's bench high above the floor, and big windows that let in plenty of natural sunlight that reflected off the cool chromium of the courtroom's floors. Kiley spotted Sid and Serenity in the second row. Bruce was sitting with the colonel and Susan several rows back. Tom was near them.

"Do you think Mommy will win?" Serenity asked as Kiley slid in beside her.

Kiley mustered up the most reassuring smile she could. "Of course she will, sweetie. You'll be seeing her in no time."

She wished she could believe it as much as it sounded like she did.

She was about to offer more reassuring—if vacant—words, when a hefty bailiff with bald spots stomped in from a rear door and stood at attention in front of the judge's bench. "Oyez, oyez, oyez. Silence is commanded on pain of imprisonment while the honorable Judge Timothy Terhune of the Superior Court of the State of California enters the room. All rise."

Judge Terhune entered, swung his gavel into the bench like a hatchet, shuffled some papers, and then addressed the gallery. "Now, before we begin, I know this is a particularly high-profile case, so I want to make perfectly clear that this court will disallow the use of any and all photography. And there are no televisions in this courtroom, as you can see. This is a *closed court*." He surveyed the room to let the statement's gravity sink in. "We're not trying to draw an iron curtain here, but I don't want to be accused of turning the courtroom into a three-ring circus."

The gallery nodded solemnly. "So as long as we can maintain some decorum, I think the proceedings will go smoothly. Thank you. Bailiff, the defendant, please."

Another bailiff opened the rear door. Platinum entered, with Richie Singleton at her right hand and his team of supporting lawyers in tow. She looked as vigilant as the figurehead on a ship, her solemn face preparing for the trial.

So much for Judge Terhune's appeal for restraint. The courtroom thundered its applause for the celebrity defendant.

Judge Terhune hammered his gavel until the clapping died down. "Order! Order! Will the defendant please take her seat?"

He waited patiently until Platinum turned from the gallery and gracefully sat. "In the case of the State of California versus Ms. Rhonda Jones." Laughter overtook the last part of his sentence, and Terhune was forced to wait until the hilarity of Platinum's little-known legal name had washed through the courtroom. "Is the prosecution ready for its opening statement?"

5

"Today marked the first day of the Platinum child-endangerment and drug trial at the Beverly Hills courthouse. Let's go to Maria-José Escalera for a summary of the day's proceedings. Maria-José?"

The television picture shifted to the courthouse steps, where a beautiful, slender Latina reporter with perfectly arched brows and too much maroon lip gloss was reporting. Esme edged closer to a television suspended over the bar at Deep South, the popular cowboy/country music club in the heart of Hollywood. This club was the venue of the wrap party for *Montgomery,* the set-in-the-Deep-South small-town indie picture in which Jonathan Goldhagen had a major role.

Though by Hollywood standards the movie was low budget—in the six- or seven-million-dollar range—the wrap party itself was lavish. There was a chuckwagon buffet, a five-piece country band rocking the house, two mechanical bulls set up inside a small corral of hay bales, and what seemed like the cast, crew, and families of several indie movies and one or two studio blockbusters in attendance. Most everyone was clad in western wear for the party, except for Esme. She'd worn black jeans with white stitching, a black tank top, and one of Jonathan's custom-made white cotton dress shirts over it, knotted just above her waist. She just couldn't see herself in chaps and a cowboy hat.

Jonathan stepped up behind her; she felt him put his strong arms around her. She leaned into him. "Watching the news?"

"Shhh." Esme really wanted to hear. "It's about Kiley's boss."

"Okay, okay. Let's check it out. Then let's mingle."

They listened as the reporter briefly described the day's proceedings in the courtroom and the media circus outside. Since the judge was not permitting cameras in the courtroom, it was up to reporters like this one to give their impressions of the testimony and the lawyers' performances. As Jonathan and Esme watched, Escalera waxed poetic about both the prosecution's and the defense's opening statement, and related that actual testimony would start the day after tomorrow because the judge had previously scheduled a minor medical procedure.

"The nature of that medical procedure is still a mystery, but Judge Terhune assured the lawyers and the jury that he'd be back in court on Wednesday. This is Maria-José Escalera, Eyewitness News."

The moment the broadcast was over, Esme saw a cowboyhatted, bandanna-wearing bartender point a remote at the TV and switch it over to the end of the Dodgers' game with the Mets.

So much for interest in the real *news of the day,* Esme thought.

Jonathan lifted Esme's hair and brushed his fingertips across the back of her neck, making her shudder. In a good way. "How's Kiley doing?" he asked.

"I think okay, I haven't talked to her since— Hey, there she is. Let's go ask her."

Kiley had just stepped into the bar area with her boyfriend, Tom.

"Tell you what, I've got to go check in with my director. I haven't seen him all night," Jonathan said, then patted his pants for his phone. "Get the coverage, text me, and I'll hook up with you when the speeches begin."

Esme was mildly disappointed that Jonathan didn't want to hang out with her, but she understood. Movies were a business, just like nannying or tattooing. There were things you wanted to do and things you had to do. The things you had to do always came first. Tonight, the thing that Jonathan had to do was put on a good show for everyone associated with his movie.

"No problem." She stood on tiptoe—Jonathan was easily six foot two—and kissed him, then watched him in his faded Levi's and checkered shirt as he threaded through the thick crowd into the main room of the club. Meanwhile, she saw Kiley and Tom working their way over to her.

"How's my favorite non-felon?" Esme quipped.

Her friend sighed. "I don't drink, otherwise I'd be drunk."

Tom rubbed Kiley's neck sympathetically. "I'm gonna get myself a beer. You want anything?"

The way Tom touched Kiley made Esme smile. So many times, Kiley had worried about whether Tom was into Kiley as much as she was into him. That gentle touch answered that question, so long as Kiley was secure enough to listen to it.

47

"Just a Coke, I guess," Kiley told Tom as he moved off to the bar.

"Coke it is."

Esme couldn't help admiring the rear view as Tom sidled up to the bartender. "Looking good."

"Imagine," Kiley joked, "that *and* a hundred thousand dollars."

Esme raised her eyebrows. "Someone is paying you a hundred thousand dollars to date someone that hot? Sign me up."

"It isn't like that." Kiley frowned, then quickly explained how she'd been approached outside the courthouse by an editor from the *Universe* and offered six figures to tell her story to the magazine.

"Damn," Esme said. "Are you going to do it?"

"Do what?"

Esme and Kiley turned. There was Lydia, in the shortest Daisy Duke cutoffs Esme had ever seen, an old Houston Oilers football jersey that had been chopped practically to nothing with scissors or a knife, and a straw cowboy hat that would have looked stupid on almost anyone else but that was astonishingly sexy on her.

"Hey, y'all. Before you ask—yes, I'm here with Billy. I didn't get a chance to thank you properly, Esme. So here are some Amazon-style thanks." With those words, she flung herself into Esme's arms with so much enthusiasm that Esme was literally rocked back on her heels.

Esme was not used to being grabbed like that, and frankly, she didn't like it. On the other hand, she really liked Lydia. "You're welcome. Where's Billy, then?"

Lydia chucked her chin toward the main room. "Back there

someplace. He's friends with the production designer on Jonathan's movie. I think they're networking." She turned to Kiley. "So who are you going to do?"

Esme had to laugh. For a girl who had very little actual sexual experience, Lydia certainly talked about it a lot. "Believe it or not, we weren't talking about sex. It was about money."

Lydia grinned. "Two subjects near and dear to my heart. Do tell, Kiley."

One more time, Kiley told the story of the magazine guy from the *Universe* who had offered her all the money for her story.

"You're going to do it, aren't you?" Lydia's head swiveled as a chiseled, barechested African American guy in cowboy chaps strode by.

"How can I?" Kiley asked. "It's not my story to tell."

Lydia pulled down the brim of her cowboy hat and exaggerated her drawl. "It's like this, sweet pea. Y'all are gonna fess up on the witness stand for free anyway. Why not get some benefit from it?"

"Because it's just . . . it's not right," Kiley insisted.

Tom came back from the bar with a cardboard tray of Cokes and a couple of Lone Star beer bottles. Lydia immediately took one of the beers and hoisted it in Kiley's direction. "Does your boyfriend know what a good person you are, Kiley?"

"Yes, I do," Tom replied. "Sometimes too good." He lifted a Lone Star of his own to Kiley.

"Did she tell you she's passing up a hundred thousand bucks for about an hour's work?" Lydia pressed.

Tom reached for Kiley's hand. "She can tell me all about it while we go dance. Do you know how to two-step, Kiley?"

Kiley reddened slightly. "Not a clue."

"Time to learn. Excuse us." He led Kiley off in the same direction that Jonathan had departed earlier.

Lydia sighed. "That boy looks good coming *and* going."

The party was getting truly raucous now, with huge whoops and shouts coming from the main room, and the country band putting enough drive in their music to have it edge dangerously toward rock and roll.

"I've got a great idea!" Lydia shouted over the pounding beat.

"What?" Esme said.

"Let's dance, too!" Lydia grabbed Esme's hand and yanked her toward the dance floor, where they were soon surrounded by the young and the beautiful. Dancing with another girl wasn't at all strange to Esme—when she and her ex-boyfriend, Junior, went to the salsa clubs in east Los Angeles, Esme and her girlfriends would dance all the time—but dancing to twangy country was another thing entirely. The lead singer was singing a song about mixing Southern rock and country, but Esme just couldn't get into the music.

"What's the matter?" Lydia, who immediately had started boogying to the music as if she'd grown up on it, instead of on Amazonian tribal chants, stopped dancing.

"These aren't my tunes. I'm taking a break."

"Could you go buy me a bottle of real expensive champagne?" Lydia asked over the music.

"It's an open bar," Esme pointed out. "It's all free."

Lydia bumped her hip into Esme's. "I'm foolin'. But just out of curiosity, rich girl, how much money did Jacqueline pay for her tattoo last night?"

"Too much. I'll be back."

Esme snaked her way through the crowd toward the bar. Truth be told, she'd taken home fifteen hundred dollars the night before for four hours of work, plus a dinner that had been delivered by room service from the kitchen of the Polo Lounge, a landmark of the Beverly Hills Hotel. Fifteen hundred dollars— Jacqueline had been so pleased with the tattoo that she'd tipped extravagantly—was three times what Esme made at the Gold-hagens' in a week, for less than a tenth of the time invested. Every time she thought about this, she had to wonder: why in the world was she still a nanny? If her business took off, she could make three hundred thousand dollars a year for creating art.

Then she thought how disappointed her mother and father would be. "We're not working this hard so you can carve up and paint people's arms," her father had told her in Spanish when they'd had a family dinner last Saturday night at their tiny bungalow in Echo Park. "You keep this job, you go to that good school so you can be someone someday. Tattoos are for *cholos*."

Esme reached the bar. There were a half dozen people in front of her waiting to place drink orders, including two gorgeous girls who were making out. It was clear to Esme that they were doing this for show, as they kept looking around to see who was looking back. Both girls had visible tattoos. The strawberry blonde with the blunt-cut bob had a dolphin peeking out from the low-cut back of her pink silk shirt, and the brunette had a yin-yang sign on her lower back that dipped into the top of her designer jeans.

Talk about boring body art. Hell, she could probably talk those two girls into new tattoos right this minute if she wanted to. She would learn about who they were, their hopes and dreams, and design a tattoo for both of them that was one of a kind, utterly unique. Those girls would recommend her to more girls and more guys . . . and if she was really careful and saved nearly every penny, soon she would have enough money to buy her parents a decent house and get their immigration status regularized. She could always go to school later on. Was she out of her mind not to?

She felt her cell phone vibrate. Jonathan? No. It was a text from Lydia. She had met up with Billy on the other side of the stage. Did Esme want to join them?

Well, why not? She wasn't about to take a ride on one of the mechanical bulls—currently an obviously drunk girl whose breasts looked as if they could double as flotation devices was on the one nearest to the bar line. A crowd of guys stood around and watched her appreciatively.

Ugh.

Where was Jonathan, anyway? He had to be hobnobbing with the usual Hollywood insiders. Esme had about as much interest in hobnobbing as she had in getting a dolphin tattoo herself.

I'll bring drinks, Esme texted back to Lydia. *Tequila.* It took another ten minutes before Esme got to the front of the bar line. When she did, alcohol was the last thing that interested her— because she happened to glance over at the dance floor, and there on the periphery was Jonathan, dancing not with some Hollywood A-list player he needed to impress, but rather with Tarshea. The Jamaican girl looked stunningly beautiful in another outfit that Diane Goldhagen must have bought for her, because there was no way that Esme's co-nanny could have afforded it herself. She wore a fuchsia minidress by Tracy Reese—Esme knew the designer because she'd tried it on herself with Diane on a shopping expedition with the twins to the Beverly Center. But Diane didn't buy it for her, and the four-figure price tag was far too rich for Esme's tastes, tattoo business or no tattoo business.

The dress looked great. Jonathan looked great. Tarshea and Jonathan looked great together. And from the way that Tarshea was snaking her arms around Jonathan's neck, Tarshea undoubtedly felt great, too.

What was she doing here? With *Esme's* boyfriend?

It must have been the intensity of her stare that made Jonathan and Tarshea look toward her at the exact same time. Esme saw Jonathan lean forward and say something to Tarshea. The Jamaican girl nodded, then Jonathan hurried over to Esme.

"I bet you're wondering what she's doing here," he said quickly.

"No shit, Sherlock."

"Diane texted me, said that it would be good for Tarshea to meet some industry people, and dropped her off. It wasn't my call."

"Uh-huh." Esme didn't know whether to believe him or not. Especially because she could see that Tarshea was staring at the two of them with the biggest shit-eating grin on her lovely heart-shaped face.

I could deck her, Esme considered. *I could kick her ass so easily—*

"You don't believe me," Jonathan said. "Here. Look at the text."

He whipped out his iPhone and with a few practiced flicks of his finger got to a text message that indeed had come from Diane. He stuck the screen in front of Esme's face. "Believe me now?"

Esme nodded. Not that it made her feel all that much better. Since when was Jonathan Diane's puppet? He didn't even like his stepmother all that much.

"I was just surprised," Esme said, covering. No way was she going to play the jealous girlfriend.

"Well, I hope this is a surprise, too." Jonathan leaned in and kissed her. "Wait for me in the bar. I'll be there in ten minutes. I promise," he murmured when the kiss was over.

That would have been fine with Esme. Except she glanced again at Tarshea, and the girl still had the strangest look on her face, as if she knew something Esme didn't.

But no, that had to be Esme's imagination. Still, she couldn't shake the feeling that Tarshea was after her guy. No, more than that. Tarshea was after her *life*.

6

"Dang, I can't kiss all of you at once!" Lydia exclaimed to the barechested cowboy whose arms were snaked around her waist.

"You can try," his friend drawled, elbowing his way in. He nibbled on Lydia's lower lip.

Lydia smiled. "Well, I—"

"I look horrible in *everything*!" a female voice wailed.

Lydia's eyes popped open. The cowboys of her dream were gone. Damn. That was a *great* dream. Instead, her cousin Martina was standing over Lydia's bed.

"What's up, sweet pea?" Lydia asked groggily.

"Are you going to sleep *forever*?"

Why was Martina even up? Lydia turned to squint at her digital clock. Nine-thirty. Oops. That would explain Martina. Plus, Billy would be there in an hour to take Jimmy to a Dodgers game. They would get there early, for batting practice. And she was incredibly late.

She shot up in bed, immediately wishing she hadn't. The herd of stampeding wild boar in her brain was a rude reminder of how much fun she'd had at last night's movie wrap party. Also, how many Lone Stars she'd consumed. She'd been back in Billy's good graces for just a couple of days, and she'd gotten it in her mind to celebrate as though it was a coming-of-age ritual celebration for one of the Amas, complete with potions that the local shaman would blow up her nose. Instead of the potions, she'd substituted beers down her gullet. Now she was paying for it. Nothing left to do but suck it up and get moving.

"You have a hangover," Martina said knowingly as Lydia slid out of bed and staggered to her closet.

Lydia couldn't decide whether to admit it or deny it. Frankly, either choice took too much work. She blindly plucked a yellow boatnecked Marc Jacobs babydoll and the first jeans she reached for from her closet and pulled them on.

"I wish I had your figure," Martina said, sighing.

"Sweetie, you are a beautiful girl," Lydia told her. "Especially after your makeover."

She pushed into some white leather Burberry sandals, plundered from an overlooked corner of a Beverly Hills consignment store at a price she'd haggled down from the cheap to the ridiculous.

"No I'm not. I'm still fat."

"Where I come from they'd call you bony," Lydia pointed out. "Don't get hung up on this whole Hollywood skinny thing. It isn't real."

"You can't be cool if you aren't skinny," Martina insisted.

Lydia padded to the bathroom to splash some cold water on

her face, slam two extra-strength Tylenol, and brush her teeth. Martina watched her every move.

"How come you always look so perfect?" Martina asked.

Her cousin had a serious case of hero worship. If Lydia's head didn't feel as if someone was drilling into it without benefit of anesthesia, she might be flattered.

She coaxed the little girl back to the main house and headed into the kitchen, where, thankfully, a fresh pot of French roast coffee was just waiting. After she'd drained half a cup, feeling slightly more human, she let Martina drag her up to her room.

When she pushed the door open, she was assaulted by a mountain of clothing. On the floor.

"Martina? What in the heck are you doing? You need a machete just to get through this stuff."

Martina had emptied the contents of every closet, armoire, and dresser in her room onto the floor, if the floor even existed somewhere beneath the pile.

The girl anxiously twisted the material of her baggy Adidas sweatshirt. "I don't look good in any of these things. But you look really good even though you just woke up. I couldn't do that if I had all day."

Lydia knew where this was going. Martina had had body issues for quite a while now. Not that anything was wrong with her body, especially with all the exercise she'd been getting lately. It was just that the girl was naturally large boned. And she had a fully developed figure. She was never going to be a cute little wisp, and she was never going to look like the little girl she really was.

"I want to go shopping," Martina said. "I want new clothes. *Cute* clothes."

Lydia was wary. "You know they have to be age appropriate."

"That's okay!" Martina agreed quickly.

"Tell you what. Get yourself dressed, do your Russian, do your abs, and then meet me in the kitchen. I'll be waiting. If the moms say it's okay, maybe I'll take you shopping."

Martina threw her arms around Lydia, much like the way the Amas said thank you, Lydia realized. Which was kind of ironic when you thought about it.

She went down to the kitchen, poured herself a second cup of coffee, and got some sliced papaya and mango from the fridge. For once, there was no list on the kitchen table giving a moment-by-moment, blow-by-blow preview of how she should occupy the kids' time for the day. Of course, Anya knew that Billy was coming to take Jimmy to the Dodgers game. And Martina was old enough to know what she had to do without being told. For the next forty-five minutes, Lydia luxuriated in the freedom of the morning *Los Angeles Times,* last week's *People,* and Kat's (not Anya's) *Vogue.* She was deep into an article about the coming winter's fashions when the doorbell rang.

Billy. She realized her headache was gone.

She hustled to the door, but found she'd been beaten by someone even more excited to see Billy than she was. Jimmy. Either he was quaking with excitement or that boy really had to pee.

Lydia guessed it might be both. Excitement did that to a person, and Jimmy had been anticipating today's Dodgers game with every passing minute since he'd learned he was going. When she reached the door, Billy—dressed in jeans, a white T-shirt, and a Dodgers cap—was deep in conversation with Jimmy about today's starting pitchers, the expected crowd at

Dodger Stadium, how many Dodger Dogs Jimmy would be permitted to eat and to watch batting practice in order to have the best chance of snaring a major league baseball.

Jimmy thrust something the size and shape of a hairless squirrel monkey at her. "Look what Billy got me!"

As Lydia looked at the baseball glove, Billy leaned over and gave her a soft kiss on the mouth. "And good morning to you."

"Ugh, I'm never kissing," Jimmy stated.

"Yeah, well, I'll check in on that sentiment in five or six years," Billy said, chuckling. "I'm guessing you'll change your mind."

"Nope." Jimmy folded his arms.

Billy smiled at Lydia. "I got him a catcher's mitt. It's not for the game; hard to catch a foul ball with it. I'll bring another glove—a fielder's glove. But this one's signed by Mike Piazza."

"Who's Mike Piazza?" Lydia asked.

Jimmy looked incredulous. "He's only the best hitter and catcher the Dodgers ever had, 1992 to 1998. Jeez. Don't you know *anything*?"

"I guess not," Lydia replied, because anything at which Jimmy felt as if he was an authority could only be good for the kid.

Just then, Martina vaulted down the stairs, uncharacteristically sporty in a black tank top that was only one size too big instead of three, and jeans that were not, in fact, swimming on her. "Hi, Billy! Do you think—"

Unfortunately, her grand entrance was snuffed out by an audio fireworks display that erupted in the kitchen. Judging by the volume, there was trouble in paradise between the moms.

"For you is completely different situation," Anya ranted in

her Muscovite accent. "You go from tennis match to tennis match. Always on road. Different city, different people. Is never any problem."

"You don't think I'd stay home if I could? You know how much I hate traveling. Don't try and confuse the issue."

"We take this to bedroom!"

"Fine. That's the only thing you seem to be taking to the bedroom these days."

Lydia exchanged a pained look with Billy. She put a comforting hand on Martina's back and could feel the little girl stiffen. Jimmy was staring at the slate floor. Having your parents fight, whether it was Mom and Dad or Mom and Mom, was a painful thing. Didn't Kat and Anya realize how their fighting made the kids feel? Lydia might have had to play the moderator, but that didn't make her impartial. She was on her aunt's side a hundred percent. She reminded herself to have that conversation with Anya. It wouldn't do any good to put it off any longer.

"Ready to go to the game?" Billy asked Jimmy.

"Totally."

Lydia made a quick decision. Martina could do the rest of her Russian and everything else on her morning schedule later. "Ready to go shopping?" Lydia asked her cousin.

Martina smiled gratefully. Lydia was happy she could give her that much, at least.

Escorting Martina down the boutique-lined sidewalks of Montana Avenue in Santa Monica was doubly thrilling. Not only was it a new experience for Lydia (on her tight budget, except for the occasional supersale, Montana Avenue was a forbidden zone). But watching Martina rubberneck as she passed each shop window was as cool as watching a newborn capybara open its eyes for the first time.

"Ooh. Let's go in this one." Martina pointed to a shop called Swank. Two writer types—five o'clock shadows, T-shirts, torn jeans, and baseball caps—the only visible difference between them and street people was the telltale laptop cases slung over their shoulders—flanked the door on competing cell phone calls.

Lydia hesitated, because the clothes in Swank's window were much too sexy for her cousin. Besides, after reaching Kat on her phone and getting permission to use her ATM code to withdraw some serious cash for their shopping extravaganza, they'd already arranged to have half a dozen shopping bags full of new clothes delivered to the house so that they wouldn't have to lug them around. She *could* just say no. But the look on Martina's face was so hopeful.

"Well, we can look," Lydia decided.

They had scarcely opened the door when they were approached by a blond salesgirl in three-inch-heeled orange suede boots and a yellow crocheted minidress that barely covered the thong panties the girl might or might not have been wearing. Lydia loved the dress—she would definitely wear it herself. But on her ten-year-old cousin? She glanced over at Martina, who was eyeing the girl's dress pretty much the way Lydia figured Juliet must have looked at Romeo.

"Hi, welcome to Swank! My name's Melanie. But you can just call me Mel." Her voice had a throaty, sexy quality. "So you guys are sisters, right?" she guessed. "Which sister are we looking for?"

"Cousin," Lydia corrected. Martina had already gravitated to a rack of leather miniskirts in Day-Glo colors.

"She's ten," Lydia added for Mel's benefit.

"Oh, but I'm sure she wants to look older," Mel said easily. "All the little girls do now. It's so cute."

"Wow, look at this!" Martina was holding up a leopard-print bustier with various snaps and zippers that seemed alarmingly primed for a wardrobe malfunction.

"Oh yeah, I love that one!" Mel exclaimed. "It would look so cute on you!"

"About eight years from now," Lydia added, giving the sales-girl a pointed look. How had her cousin gone from no-show to show-off so quickly? What weird social cues had given her the idea that it would be good to dress the age of her body rather than the age she actually was?

"Well, I like it," Martina said defiantly.

"If we brought that home, the moms would never let you come shopping with me again," Lydia said.

With a dramatic sigh, Martina put the bustier back. Mel correctly guessed Martina's size and brought her some jeans to try on, extreme low-rise. Lydia was pretty sure the moms would nix them, but maybe she could persuade Martina to match them with a T-shirt long enough to cover the inches of stomach the jeans would bare. Martina disappeared into the dressing room with the first pair.

Lydia watched two girls stroll in with Fred Segal shopping bags. They had the same haircut and the same superskinny bodies. They actually looked nothing alike, but they'd styled themselves into some kind of L.A.-generic hip look. How awful, Lydia decided, to try to look like everyone else.

"How's it going in there?" she called to Martina.

"Almost . . . on." From inside the dressing room, Martina groaned. "I'm still so fat!" she yelled.

"Sweet pea, you are not fat."

"I can't even zip these up."

"That's because you have hips," Lydia explained patiently through the door. "Girls are supposed to have hips."

"No, they're not!"

Lydia could hear the tears in Martina's voice.

"Come on, honey bun. Get dressed. We'll get X to drive us over to Fred Segal. Their clothes are much cooler," Lydia insisted. And they carried a wide-enough variety that her little cousin wouldn't try to stuff herself into tiny jeans, or lust after clothes that were all wrong for her.

When Martina came out, red-faced, she thrust the jeans back at Mel. "Nothing fit."

Mel shrugged. "Gee, those jeans don't come any bigger."

Lydia wanted to smack her. "The clothes in here are just too tacky for words," she said coolly. "Come on, Martina. Let's shop somewhere else."

Lydia already had her cell out and was punching in X's number as they walked out the door.

They spent an hour at Fred Segal, and bought Martina a pretty paisley blouse, a pink cashmere sweater, and two pairs of sandals. The little girl was in a much better mood when X dropped them off back home. The packages from the various stores had already been delivered and sat in the front hallway.

"We're back!" Martina shouted as they stepped inside. No answer. Huh. The guys must still have been at the stadium; Anya and Kat had to be out.

"Why don't you put your new clothes away? I'll bring up some smoothies and we can toss out the old stuff."

"That sounds great!" Martina exclaimed. "Can we burn them?"

"In the Amazon, the Amas used to burn their old clothes in a sort of purification rite. I don't think the air pollution people here would be too thrilled, though. Let's just give them to Goodwill. Not everyone has money for new clothes."

"That's a good idea."

Martina bounded off to the stairs, and Lydia headed for the kitchen. With any luck, the moms' chef, Paisley, would still be on duty and could whip up some five-fruit smoothies. "Paisley? Are you—"

Lydia froze in her tracks just inside the kitchen door. Paisley wasn't there. But her aunt Kat was. And she looked a mess. In fact, she turned her face away and blotted at her eyes with a white cloth napkin.

"Aunt Kat? Are you okay?"

"No." She blew her nose and wiped her reddened eyes.

Lydia got a bottle of Fiji water from the fridge and brought it to her aunt, then stood by, ready to console her. It didn't take a genius to put together what had happened. Confirmation came from Kat soon enough.

"I got a call about Anya," Kat finally said. "A friend from the club saw her with some *man*. Some army guy. I think he's Platinum's brother-in-law. They were kissing in a golf cart behind some storage shed near the eleventh hole. My friend had hooked a shot and was searching for the ball. He found them instead."

So it was true. Anya and the colonel. Whoa. And Lydia hadn't had to tell Kat, or talk to Anya about it either. Kat knew. The question now was, what was her aunt going to do about it?

"So . . . I asked Anya about it."

"What did she say?" Lydia chose her words carefully.

"She told me she didn't think she was gay anymore and maybe never was. And she said . . . she said that she didn't love me."

"Where is she now?"

"I don't know. Not here. Someplace else. I think a bungalow at the Beverly Hills Hotel. Or . . ." Kat could barely continue. "You have to help me tell the kids, okay? I don't think I can break this to them alone."

Lydia nodded soberly. "I'm so sorry. I will do whatever you need for the kids. They heard some arguing this morning, but I don't—"

Just then, they heard the front door swing open.

"Hey! Who's home?" Jimmy called.

Lydia saw her aunt pale. She squeezed her hand. "Are you okay?"

Kat nodded. "I'll pull it together. I promise."

"Take as much time as you need. Like I said, I got it covered," Lydia assured her. She slapped a smile on her face and strode out to the foyer. "Hey, you two. How was the game?"

"It was so cool," Jimmy said, his eyes shining. "We sat right by the dugout, and we got Jeff Kent to sign my glove, and we got some hot dogs, and we yelled at the Padres' pitcher, and he looked right at us, right, Billy?"

Billy nodded. "If he's lying, I'm dying."

"And the Dodgers won eight to two!" Jimmy finished triumphantly.

Billy held up a large hand, and the little boy high-fived him.

"That's fantastic." Lydia tried to sound enthusiastic, but all she could think was: How could she possibly prepare this kid for the catastrophic letdown that was about to descend on his head? Divorce sucked for kids, and it didn't matter if it was a dad and a mom or two moms.

Lydia looked to Billy, who was obviously thrilled by Jimmy's enthusiasm. She could have used his help on this one. But barring telepathy, there was no good way of telling him. "You just made his year." That was the best she could do.

"It was nothing. The Mets are coming next week. Want to go again, Jimmy?"

Before Jimmy could exult at the invitation, Kat stepped over to them with a wan smile.

"I don't mean to interrupt, Lydia, but could you and the kids meet me in the living room as soon as you can?" She turned and hurried off, not meeting her son's eyes.

"What's wrong with Momma Kat?" Jimmy asked.

Lydia wasn't surprised. Kids picked up on any kind of problem with their parents so easily.

"Let's go talk to her and find out," Lydia suggested. She kissed Billy goodbye and promised to call him later. Billy reiterated his promise to take Jimmy to the Mets game; then he left. Lydia had to get Martina and take both kids in to face the bad news.

Man. This was gonna suck.

7

"Runners, take your marks. . . ."

Kiley dug her fingertips into the artificial rubber surface of the running track at Bel Air High School. The athletics director, Bucky Shelton, who'd made a big deal of the fact that he'd played football at USC and then for the San Francisco 49ers before he retired and became an educator, had explained this was the same surface used at the Olympic games.

Kiley did not care. Kiley did not like to run. In fact, Kiley *hated* running. She felt as fast and graceful cutting through the water as she felt slow and ungainly galumphing along while the fleet-footed left her in the dust. But it wasn't as if she had a choice. All the students were required to do athletic testing before the new semester began. And this was the day they were doing it.

"Get set. . . ."

She glanced quickly to her left. Along with the other six or seven girls in the starting blocks, who looked as if they wanted to be there about as much as she did, which was to say not at all, was Zona, the pixieish one of the three obnoxious girls who'd given her a tour of the high school during that first day of orientation. To her right was Lydia, in the same blue shorts/white BAHS T-shirt that everyone else had been given, but in bare feet instead of running shoes. Lydia claimed before the race that she ran faster in bare feet. The athletic director had looked at her cockeyed, then gave a dismissive shrug and motioned Lydia to the starting blocks.

Crack!

The starter pistol sounded, and the race began. Four hundred meters, about a quarter of a mile, one complete circuit of the track. Kiley was not the kind of girl to give up before she even started, so she tucked her elbows in and gave it her all. She cut her eyes at Zona, who was already behind her. Kiley hoped Zona would finish last. Not that Zona had given any indication of being the kind of girl who cared about anything like doing your best, but it would still be satisfying to beat her. She bet that Lydia would—

Whoa. In the space of a split second, barefoot Lydia flashed past her, a blur of platinum blond hair and churning coltlike legs. Quickly, Lydia had a ten-yard lead, and soon after that, thirty, then fifty yards. Kiley chugged along as fast as she could. She found herself in the middle of the pack—not as bad as she'd anticipated. When she rounded the rest of the track, she could see Zona not far from the starting blocks, walking. Well, Kiley wasn't surprised. Girls like her thought acting as if they were too cool to try rendered them even more fabulous. Kiley found the attitude monumentally annoying.

Up ahead, Lydia was nearing the finish line. Kids were

actually cheering her. A huge roar went up when she crossed the line that ended the race.

Mr. Shelton's voice boomed out over a bullhorn. "The rest of you keep running! Miss Chandler just did the four hundred in fifty-one fifty-two! That's an unofficial school record. Woo-hoo!"

By the time Kiley finished—thankfully, not last—there was a crowd of people gathered around Lydia, who stood by the finish line. They were firing questions at her. Where had she gone to middle school? Had she ever competed in track and field before? How was she in sprints? Long distance? And from Coach Shelton—"I'm going to make you into a star, Miss Chandler!"

It amused Kiley to see Lydia deflect all the queries. "There's nothing that makes you run faster than a wild boar chasing you through the bush," she told the group matter-of-factly.

"You are going to be Bel Air High's star runner," Mr. Shelton enthused. "We are about to put this school on the map for girls' track and field!"

"Like we care," Kiley heard Zona mutter as she laconically walked past the finish line and joined the group.

"Well, I don't know that I'm interested," Lydia replied, quite honestly. "However, if I was going to be interested, you'd have to actually ask me," she added sweetly.

Instead of taking offense, Coach Shelton just handed Lydia a clean towel, which Lydia simply slung around her neck because she wasn't sweating.

"I hope you will consider going out for track and field, Miss Chandler," the coach said. "It would mean a lot to me and your student-athlete classmates if you'd try out for the track team. I assure you that we've got a spot for you. Any event you want to run."

"That is just so sweet of you," Lydia gushed. "I'll think about it."

Mr. Shelton smiled. "Great! Fantastic! I know you'll decide to go ahead with this. Just think about how it will look on your college—"

Lydia held up a hand. "Excuse me, but I'm done thinking. I'm afraid the answer is no. When I run, I like to run for a reason, not a ribbon. My idea of outdoor aerobic activity is shopping at the Grove."

All around her, girls giggled and cast admiring glances her way. Meanwhile, Coach Shelton's beefy face turned tomato red.

"B-but you could get an athletic scholarship with your talent. You could go to Stanford!"

"Well, see, I'm not even sure I want to go to college. But thanks for the encouragement."

With that declaration, Lydia nodded politely and then started walking away, to applause from the crowd. No one was objecting; no one was imploring Lydia to run track because the whole school would be oh-so-proud. Clearly, athletics here at Bel Air High School were nothing like at La Crosse, where the guy athletes were venerated and even the girls got a lot of attention, especially if they were swimmers or volleyball players. Getting another big championship banner up in the gym, or a trophy for the trophy case, was a reason for a school assembly. Here in Bel Air, it seemed like an anti-achievement.

"Come on, Kiley," Lydia told her. "Walk with me. We can't leave until we're officially dismissed, I think. Lord, they've got some dumb-ass rules."

Kiley stepped alongside her friend; they headed across the track and toward the bleachers. These seats were padded, just like the ones in the basketball arena, and had the additional benefit of an overhang that protected fans from the sun. It was a remarkably pleasant place to hang out, so different from the harsh cold steel bleachers in the football stadium at La Crosse East High School. Kiley remembered how, one year, the annual Thanksgiving Day football game against Eau Claire was played in fifteen-below weather and several fans were taken to the hospital with frostbite. "That was amazing. How you ran before."

Lydia brushed off the accolades with a wave of her hand. "What I said about the wild boar? This one time, one of them got so close I could feel him breathing on me. I jumped up, grabbed a vine, and swung into a tree."

"How Tarzan of you," Kiley remarked. "So then what happened?"

"Eventually Snout Boy lumbered away. But it took quite a while. I'd read an article that week in *Complete Woman* about how running makes your butt real perky—it was the only magazine I had. The Amas liked to steal them. And then there was that pesky problem with no toilet paper, and pages of magazines work real well, so—"

"The wild boar?" Kiley prompted.

"Right, the boar. Like I said, the boar got bored. But right then, I decided I'd have to be a complete woman without running around some little track. Running to save your life from a rabid boar—that's a different story. And I like my ass just the way it is."

Kiley laughed. That was just so Lydia.

Lydia blocked the sun with a hand to her forehead and peered around the field. "Have you seen Esme?"

Kiley motioned toward the far end of the field. Though many of the hundreds of seniors who'd come to the high school this morning for their athletics pretesting—the school grouped its physical education classes by ability—had drifted away into little knots, or had plopped down on the grass to sun themselves, there were still a few groups at the other end doing strength testing. Kiley had already been through that station. It involved sit-ups, push-ups, and a softball throw. She hadn't been very good at any of it.

"I saw her down there. She didn't look very happy."

"Now see, that I do not understand," Lydia said. "She's got the hot guy and the hot gig. Plus the rich and famous are throwin' major bucks at her to ink little designs into their skin. That's a danged sweet situation if you ask me." She twirled a lock of pale blond hair absentmindedly. "Speaking of major bucks, have you made up your mind?"

Kiley knew Lydia was referring to the tell-all offer from the *Universe*. She scratched some kind of bug bite on her forearm. "No."

"No?" Lydia echoed. "Did you drop about fifty IQ points while I was hightailing my perky butt around that track?"

Kiley put her red-checkered hightops up on the bleacher step below her. "It's just not ethical."

Lydia nodded slowly. "Hmmmm. I see your point. You don't want to profit from Platinum's problem."

"Exactly," Kiley agreed, pleased that Lydia understood.

"So do the story and give *me* the money," Lydia concluded sweetly.

Kiley laughed. "I should have known you had an angle."

Lydia elbowed her in the ribs. "Heads up. Here comes my fan club."

Kiley did a mental eye-roll as Staci and Zona bounded toward

72

them. Staci's dark locks were pushed back off her face with a slender headband, while Zona's blond curls were noticeably sweaty.

"You were fantastic!" Staci gushed to Lydia, pretty much ignoring Kiley's existence. "No one tells Coach Bucky to go to hell."

"Mr. Shelton, you mean?"

"That's what everyone calls him," Zona explained. "Only after what you said, we should call him Shell-shocked Shelton." She giggled. "I took a photo of him on my phone right after you told him to go screw himself." She held her phone out to Lydia.

Kiley leaned in to look at it. Coach Bucky's mouth was hanging open like a beached carp on the shore of the Mississippi. It really *was* funny.

"Watch out," Zona warned. "Coach Bucky will probably handcuff you to a locker until you agree to run track for him."

"If a guy is going to cuff me, it's going to be for fun," Lydia commented, "which lets ole Bucky-Boy out. Plus, he'll be younger, hotter, and up all night," Lydia drawled. She looked thoughtful. "What a fun idea. I'll have to tell Billy, my boyfriend. Where do you actually buy handcuffs—anyone know?"

The Bel Air girls' jaws dropped.

"I'm into whips and chains, myself," Kiley managed to say without blushing. She truly disliked these girls. It was fun to shock them.

Staci arched a brow. "You?" she asked dubiously.

"Oh, she's much wilder than she looks," Lydia put in.

"Where did you say you grew up again?" Zona asked. "Michigan?"

"Wisconsin."

"Whatever." Staci flipped her dark hair. "Aren't people from Wisconsin called cheeseheads?"

Zona laughed. "What a great nickname for you!" she told Kiley. "Cheesehead!"

Kiley's face burned. But what burned her even more was the fact that she was letting these two mean little bitches get to her.

"I was in Wisconsin last summer," Staci added. "My dad runs Uprising Studios. I was a production assistant on Julia Roberts's last movie—we shot in Green Bay. Frankly, I think she's toast since she became a mother."

"Totally," Zona agreed. "Zero sex appeal." She cut her eyes at Kiley. "Kind of like you, Cheesehead."

"I don't think you want to go around dissing my friend," Lydia said, her tone sweet and conversational. "Because that would make me mad. And trust me, you don't want to make me mad."

Kiley's face burned. "I can stick up for myself."

"We were only joking," Staci insisted. She stood. "We just wanted to say you kicked ass with Coach Bucky. You're going to fit in really well."

Zona stood, too. "Tell her about the football game."

Staci glared at her friend. "I was just about to do that. Lydia, there's a home game on Friday night. Our team is playing Echo Park—total lowlife greaseball gangbangers. I know it's before school actually starts, but they get going early. A lot of us go to the games and then go party. You should come and hang out with us and our friends."

Football games. Kiley never would have expected them to be social events here in California. Back in Wisconsin, Friday night football was huge. Huh. At least one thing was the same. Of

74

course, at home she went to football games with her friends. She could not imagine becoming friends with these two toxic twits.

"That sounds like fun, y'all," Lydia replied. "Kiley and I would love to come. And our friend Esme, too. Wouldn't we, Kiley?" Lydia batted her lashes.

"Not really," Kiley replied honestly. She knew the batting-the-eyelashes thing had been added as a joke, to josh Kiley into saying yes.

"Oh, you'll change your mind," Lydia insisted.

"Lucky us," Staci mumbled. She tossed her hair, then spoke to Lydia again. "Remember, we're going out afterward, so dress to impress." The toxic twits started down the bleachers.

"My first high school football game!" Lydia exclaimed. "How fun is that gonna be?"

"I would rather gnaw off my arm than go with those two," Kiley said, cocking her chin in the direction of the departing girls.

"Oh sure, they're snobs and all," Lydia agreed easily. "But not to worry. A clique is just a tribal thing. They don't want to admit new girls into their tribe. Dissing you is a rite-of-passage kind of thing. At least you don't have to drink sheep piss." She stood and yanked Kiley to her feet. "Come on. Let's tell Esme about the game."

Lydia started down the bleachers, but Kiley hung back. She'd just realized something. Hadn't Staci just said that Bel Air High was playing Echo Park? Echo Park was Esme's old school.

8

Esme had never been so thankful to see the gate to the Gold-hagens' Bel Air estate come into view. She punched in the security code, watched as the wrought-iron doors groaned open, and engaged all eight cylinders of the Goldhagens' Jaguar for the seemingly endless climb up the driveway—more like a private road, really—to the ginormous mansion.

After the field-day tryouts at school, her legs felt like Jell-O, each pulse of the crankshaft reminding her of the wind sprints she'd suffered, and the sit-ups she could barely do. She was hardly a wimp. In fact, she felt certain she could—and would, if the occasion called for it—kick the ass of any of those over-privileged brats she'd met on the field today. But sports were not her thing.

She pulled up in front of the garage, between Diane's new Mercedes and the red Jensen Interceptor that Steven had been driving lately. There were a half dozen more spotless, shiny vehicles in the garage, she knew. By the time she got out, Easton and Weston were trotting up to her. They each wore shorts and tennis shirts—Easton's outfit was pink, Weston's was yellow—and their grins were covered with barbecue sauce, like two stubby clowns who had run out of makeup.

"Esme! Esme! Come to eat chicken!" Weston implored, taking hold of one of Esme's hands with hers, which, Esme saw, were also covered in barbecue sauce, meaning that now so was she.

"Tarshea makes jerk!" Easton was practically jumping up and down with joy and excitement. She took Esme's other hand. "Come on."

Esme could certainly smell the cooking. But *Tarshea makes jerk*? Well, Esme was rapidly deciding that perhaps Tarshea *was* a jerk. Maybe the twins had come around to realizing it.

"Okay," Esme told them. "Let's go check out the jerk."

With the twins still holding her hands in their own sticky, barbecue-sauced fingers, Esme made her way down the path toward the tennis court. It was only a hundred feet from her guesthouse. Mental correction: the guesthouse she now shared with a most unwelcome guest named Tarshea.

Esme thought she'd take home-field advantage and speak a little Spanish with the girls. She asked them, in Spanish, if they missed her when she was away for the morning.

"Tarshea say we speak English. No Spanish." Easton was adamant.

Weston nodded. "English. Mom say do what Tarshea say."

"Tarshea is my teacher," Easton intoned. "Tarshea is a good teacher."

"We learn to say this," Weston explained. "We say good?"

"Very good!" Esme assured them, though inwardly she was

77

more than irritated. She'd been working on the kids' English for weeks, and now Diane was giving all the credit to the new girl? Aargh. It was just so annoying. Well, Diane and Steven would see her with the twins now, and maybe that would remind Diane that—

Esme stopped suddenly, even as the twins jerked her forward. There had been some construction done that morning. Next to the tennis court, as if it had been there for months, stood a twenty-foot-tall mahogany outdoor pavilion, complete with shingled roof, bench seating for twelve, and an accompanying Jamaican-style open fire pit. Sitting in the pavilion were Diane and Steven. Each of them was holding a Red Stripe beer, casually chatting with their guests. With them was Hilary Swank—Esme recognized her, but not her date—and a half dozen other guests. She squinted. Was that Carlos Santana? Esme was pretty sure it was. Her heart flip-flopped. Santana was her parents' favorite musician. Did her parents know? Had they met him?

She didn't see Jonathan, but over by the jerk barbecue pit, beaming beneath a chef's hat and apron and hailing Esme with a pair of tongs, was Tarshea. She wore khaki shorts and a simple white T-shirt, and she looked gorgeous.

"Come turn the jerk, children!" Tarshea beckoned to the twins, who wriggled from Esme's hands and sprinted toward the pavilion. As they did, Diane gave Esme a little wave.

"Esme! Good to see you. I'm sure the day at your high school was a nice break," Diane cooed.

Hardly. Esme just clenched a grin in response as Diane introduced her friends. "And this is one of our wonder nannies, Esme."

"Nice to meet you, Esme," Carlos said, offering her a hand-shake.

Diane laughed. "Our children are a handful. But between Esme and Tarshea, we've got the girls covered."

"Hold it, hold it. You're *the* Esme Castaneda?" the guy with Hilary—Buzz something or other—asked. "The tattoo artist?" He was medium height with an inky black Mohawk.

Esme shot a quick look at Diane to see how her employer was reacting. "Oh, it's just something I do in my spare time," she said, hoping Diane would be reassured that the tattoo thing was not interfering with the nanny thing.

"You're too modest," Buzz insisted. "I'm a huge fan of your work. I can't believe you're Diane and Steven's nanny. I never made the connection. If you have any appointments, Hil and I would love to get a session."

"Leave me your number and I'll call you," Esme said quickly. She really did not like the look on Diane's face.

"I didn't realize you were taking tattoo clients," Diane said. Her tone was conversational, but Esme could feel the frost beneath the goodwill.

"Just a few friends, really," Esme lied.

"Well," Diane said. "It's nice that you find the time." She cleared her throat. "I'm sure you want to go shower after your workout at school. Tarshea can watch the girls."

"Of course," Tarshea agreed pleasantly from the barbecue pit. "It's my favorite thing to do."

Great. Swell. Esme couldn't very well say no to a shower.

At least she had the guesthouse to herself for once. She walked in and slipped off her shoes. The cool tile felt good on her aching feet. After she'd stripped down to her bra and panties, Esme sat on her bed and opened a wooden jewelry box she'd filled with things she'd brought from the barrio: a toy horse her father had carved for her, some recipes of her grand-mother's, and some photographs. She uncovered a snapshot of herself as a grinning little girl missing her two front teeth, her fa-ther helping steady her on her first bike. They had found the bike at the Salvation Army, a broken-down thing for five dollars, and her father had managed to make it rideable. She might have been living in a better place now, but on days like these, when very little felt familiar, Esme missed the cracked slate of the Echo.

"¿Sensación nostálgica, hija mía?"

Esme looked up. There, in the doorway to the guesthouse, stood her mother, who had just asked if she was feeling home-sick.

Esmeralda Castaneda wore the crisp black uniform with white apron that Diane provided for her. Her swollen feet were encased in cheap black orthopedic shoes cracking on the sides, her hair up in a bun. She might be the Goldhagens' maid, but to Esme, her tired mother in a uniform and ugly shoes looked infi-nitely more beautiful than Diane in her designer everything.

"Sometimes," Esme confessed. She put the picture back in the box. "It's funny. You and Dad work here, but I hardly ever see you. And even if I did, seeing you here . . ." She let the rest of her sentence trail off. They would all be employees, not a fam-ily, was what she meant.

Her mother nodded, filling in the blanks. She sat beside Esme. "For you to be here and not in the Echo"—she patted the bed—"this is much better for you, *¿sí?*"

Esme knew her mom wasn't just referring to the bed itself,

but to her whole life outside Echo Park, away from the addicts, sirens, *cholos,* and gangs.

"Right," she agreed, albeit grudgingly, and pointed through the open door at the Jamaican flag now pinned to Tarshea's door. "But I feel like I'm getting pushed out by my new roommate. I come home and she's done my job already. The *niñas* prefer her. And she spends more time with the Goldhagens and the girls than I do. Even when I went to Jonathan's party, there she was."

Mrs. Castaneda gave Esme a look that Esme thought of as her evil eye. "You and that boy still?"

"I know you don't want me to see him—"

"I want you to use the brains the good Lord gave you, Esme! How many times have your father and I told you to keep clear of him?"

Esme sighed. "I know."

"Keep your place, Esme," her mother chided. "You should only hope that girl Tarshea steals him away."

Esme bristled. "My *place*?"

"I'm sorry, *mi princesita,* but you know how I feel." Her mother placed a weathered hand on Esme's knee. "And another thing. If you think it is hard to live here when you come from Echo Park, think of how hard it would be coming from another country. Without your mother or father? Without any friends? I have seen Tarshea with the kids. All she wants to do is help you, and you push her away."

Esme couldn't stand it—her mother was taking Tarshea's side, too! "You don't really know her," she insisted.

"I know why I get on my hands and knees every day to scrub the floor of the Goldhagens' bathrooms," she replied. "So that you will—"

"Have a better life," Esme filled in. Because she knew it was true. Because she'd heard it a million times.

"You waste your time worrying about the wrong things, *hija mía*," her mother gently chided. "Forget Jonathan. Forget Tarshea. Concentrate on school so you can become *somebody*."

Esme gritted her teeth. "I *am* somebody."

"*Sueños sin mucho trabajo significan nada*," her mother said.

Dreams without hard work mean nothing, her mother had just said. Which meant: Keep your eye on the ball. Not on a guy. And not on the comp.

"I'll try," she promised, then stood. "I'd better go take a shower."

Her mother stood too. "Before I go, I want to ask about your tattoo business. Are you still making money?"

Great. Why not two lectures for the price of one?

"Lots," Esme said simply.

"Your school is about to start. I don't want you too busy with other work. You got enough to do here. More than enough, *hija mía*."

Esme thought about the oh-so-charming girls she'd already met at Bel Air High, how out of place she felt there, as if she was outlined in garish, flashing neon that said POOR BROWN GIRL FROM THE WRONG SIDE OF TOWN. "It's not really my school, Mama. It's all rich white kids and no Latinos, at least none like me."

"*Nobody* is like you. You have to be strong, use it to your advantage. It may be a change from what you're used to, but this high school is your best opportunity. It's not a time for self-pity, or for tattoos. Think of your future, *mi preciosa*."

After releasing her hands, her mother hugged Esme tightly and left.

Esme took a long, steamy shower, letting the advice sink in. She'd heard it before, but Esme realized what her mother had said in a new way. She was completely correct. *Nobody* was like her. That meant nobody knew what was best for her. Nobody could tell her what to do. This conversation had been a case in point: she'd talked to the one person she could talk to, only to hear she was doing everything wrong.

Great. What a joy to think your mother believed you were totally blowing it.

She put on some black shorts with rolled-up bottoms and a simple white T-shirt and went outside again, only to find the jerk pit had been abandoned. But there was a china plate of fragrant jerk chicken and other goodies wrapped in aluminum foil with her name written in marker.

Tarshea had to have done that. It was so hard to hate someone when they were nice to you.

Where had everyone gone? After she ate half the plate of food, Esme circled around the property and discovered they'd moved to the heated pool for a rowdy game of water volleyball. The teams were evenly three on three. On one side, Easton and Weston perched themselves on the shoulders of the Hollywood couple while Steven played backcourt. On the other side, Diane took the net, with Tarshea in the back. There was one other player, too. Jonathan had arrived.

He greeted her warmly; she waved back. Esme didn't jump into the water because she didn't have her suit, and it would have made the teams uneven. Nor did anyone suggest she go put on a suit and join them. So she just stood and watched, her eyes moving to Tarshea. Perfectly toned caramel legs, displayed below the bottom of a green-and-white-polka-dotted Dolce & Gabbana bikini.

Esme's bikini.

No. She would not get angry. Instead, she dragged a patio seat to the net, and quietly suffered their exhibitions of fun and hilarity. Her gaze floated over the pool and up into the hills of Bel Air. The sky was blue and the clouds looked as though they had been painted on. The sun glinted off the sparkling blue of the pool water. While the game went on, Esme set her jaw, cupped her knees, and thought of her tattoo business. One potential design followed another, and another. Two-headed demons, symbols, and animals of every kind. On the face of every one was Jonathan and Tarshea.

9

Thursday morning at nine sharp, Kiley slipped past the assembled gaggle of pushy reporters and did her best attempt at a confident stride through the heavy wooden doors of the courthouse. She had dressed in what she thought of as "court clothes," slim black pants and ballet flats, and a robin's-egg blue button-down blouse that Lydia had found for her on sale at Nordstrom. She had taken an extra minute that morning to smooth her hair into a tidy ponytail, tucking back loose strands, knowing that people might be watching her reactions or that one of the court's sketch artists might even draw her. She made her way through security, then forced out a small smile as she walked into the courtroom, her eyes scanning the crowd for her former boss's trademark white-blond hair.

There she was, alone at the defense table.

"Kiley!" Platinum hissed and motioned to her.

Kiley weaved through a row of spectator seats and approached the singer, understated perfection in a white Chanel suit and dia-mond stud earrings. They stood together at the low wooden bar-rier between the spectators and the front of the courtroom, where the action took place.

"I am so sick of this media bullshit," Platinum groused.

This struck Kiley as ironic. The only reason she'd met Platinum in the first place was because she'd tried to do a reality show to get as much media attention as possible in an attempt to get her career off life support. It turned out that getting arrested had the same ef-fect. Ever since Platinum's sensational bust, sales of her CDs had tripled.

Platinum turned around and flashed the reporters who were gathered in the back of the courtroom a scintillating smile. No cameras were allowed in the room, but that hadn't stopped every two-bit reporter from getting press credentials. Everyone from the *New York Times* to *Us* was there. Kiley felt that they had to have more important stories to cover, but evidently they didn't agree.

"How are the kids?" Platinum asked Kiley, rapidly tapping her French-manicured fingertips against the wooden desk. "I can't believe they're putting my children on the stand. Fucking vultures."

"The kids are ready to go," Kiley assured her.

That is, she mentally amended, *if having Serenity sneak lip gloss and mascara past the colonel to apply in the courthouse's ladies' room so that she'll look good for the cameras means "ready."* All three kids were in a waiting area with a social worker who had been as-signed to them.

"I talked to my lawyer about finding some other way to make my case, but he told me there's no way around putting them on the stand," Platinum said. Anxiety clouded her eyes. "Thank God you're with them, Kiley. I really mean that."

Kiley shifted, feeling guilty. If Platinum knew that she'd been offered six figures to write a tell-all, Kiley doubted very much that she'd be praising her.

"The kids love you," she told Platinum, which was the truth. "They just want you to come home."

"Home," Platinum murmured reflectively. "God, I miss it. My room, my closets, my trainer, my Jacuzzi."

"How's detention, really?" Kiley asked.

Platinum shrugged her slim shoulders and nonchalantly tossed her waterfall of ice-pale hair. "The room service sucks, but the in-room massages are taking the edge off. How are the kids with General Asshole, also known as my sister's husband? Does he have you lining up in formation morning, noon, and night?"

"Well, it's not *quite* that bad. It was over the top for a while, but now he mostly leaves the kids to me. . . . I guess he's decided I'm trustworthy enough. He's busy golfing a lot of the time."

For a moment, she was tempted to tell Platinum just what "golfing" entailed. But this was not really the moment. Right now, Platinum needed to focus on one thing: her trial. It was so weird. Even though Kiley knew that Platinum was utterly, totally, and completely guilty, she still hoped the jury would acquit her.

"Be sure and sneak the kids some candy bars when he's not monitoring their every move. And they can watch movies on their portable DVD players in their bedrooms. They are kids, dammit. Not marines."

"Consider it done," said Kiley. A loud throat-clearing from the bailiff interrupted their conversation.

"Take your seats, guys. We're starting in three minutes." He motioned them toward their respective places.

After the loud cry of "All rise!" Judge Terhune entered the packed room in his black judicial robes, and the trial resumed. He asked the prosecutor to call his first witness.

Kiley watched Serenity, clad in khakis and a button-down blue shirt à la the colonel's instructions, head down the aisle with the social worker. Kiley stifled a laugh. Sure enough, Serenity had managed to apply lip gloss and mascara in the ladies' room. It was ridiculous on a seven-year-old, of course. But Kiley couldn't help admiring the little girl's spunk. The colonel and Susan were sitting on the aisle. When Serenity walked by him, Kiley saw his mouth tighten into a thin slash of anger that she'd defied him.

The courtroom was deadly silent as Serenity put her hand on a Bible and was sworn in, and then sat in the witness chair.

"Please begin by telling us exactly what happened on the night your mother was arrested." The prosecutor was tall, dark, and handsome, right out of a Hollywood court movie.

"It was just a normal night," Serenity said. "I was home with my brothers, Bruce and Sid, and we were all reading library books. My mom had gone out to just run some quick errands, and all of a sudden I didn't feel very good, so I called my nanny and she called the police, and then when they showed up, they arrested my mom!" She said everything in one breath, which gave her answer an urgent quality.

Kiley knew this to be total and utter bullshit. The kids did not even have library cards. Platinum never ran errands. Kiley herself had been with Platinum that night at a party aboard the *Queen Mary*.

The prosecutor turned to the judge. "Your Honor, with all due respect, this child is omitting some key details. She felt ill because she had indulged in some of her mother's marijuana, which had been left out in plain sight. Her mother wasn't out running errands; she was seen by a number of witnesses at the *Queen Mary* in Long Beach, where she was clearly intoxicated, if not under the influence of other controlled substances."

Judge Terhune looked stern. "You'll have an opportunity to prove all—"

"He can't, it's not true!" Serenity broke in, much to the delight of the gallery. "My mom just wants to stay home and take care of us! She likes to cook us dinner and help with our homework, and she doesn't even drink anymore, ever, or do drugs, *ever*—ever!"

Kiley felt horrible. Serenity was lying to protect her mother. The truth was, Platinum drank to excess all the time. She did leave marijuana around in plain sight. She loved her kids, yes. But her behavior around them was often reprehensible.

Kiley snuck a glance behind her. The colonel sat ramrod straight, his gaze fixed squarely on the witness stand. His scowl was intense. Kiley felt bad for what would happen to Serenity when she got home. She'd be confined to quarters—her room—until she was ready for the Bel Air Home for Senior Citizens.

"Young lady, I will remind you that you are under oath," the prosecutor chided. "Do you understand what that means?"

"Duh," Serenity replied, and the reporters in the back of the courtroom laughed until Judge Terhune banged his gavel for silence. "It means I have to tell the truth and I am. My mom is the best mom in the world. I don't think it's fair for you to say all this mean stuff about her. She would never do anything to hurt me, or my brothers."

Again, the prosecutor turned to the judge. Kiley wasn't sure, but it seemed as though Terhune had the hint of a smile on his face as the DA spoke. "Your Honor, there have been reports from neighbors and from former employees—nannies, cooks—that suggest a pattern of reckless behavior and abuse of alcohol on the part of the defendant. I would suggest that this young lady is lying to protect her mother."

"You don't know anything!" Serenity exclaimed, her cheeks growing red. "All those people that don't work for us anymore are mad at my mom, because she fired them for messing up at their jobs. So of course they'd say bad things about her!"

The judge asked for a sidebar with both attorneys. Kiley strained to hear, but it was impossible. So she looked over at the jury, a racially mixed group of nondescript, mostly ill-dressed men and women who clearly did not come from the neighborhood in which Platinum lived.

As the sidebar continued, Kiley felt a sharp tap on her shoulder. She turned; the colonel and Susan had moved in behind her. "Just what exactly is going on here, McCann?" demanded the colonel. "Serenity is lying and we all know it. Did you talk to her about this? It's a mockery of our country's legal system."

"I can't control what she says up there, sir," Kiley pointed out.

"Well, I can tell you one thing—when that little miss gets home, I'm going to teach her a few things about telling the truth and respecting authority. We'll see how she talks after she's spent a few weeks at my boot camp! Excuse me. I need some nonperjured air."

With another of his patented scowls, he edged away from Kiley and his wife. Kiley was left looking up at Susan, who looked . . . how, exactly? Sad. No, more than sad. Defeated.

Susan slid in next to Kiley. "Can I tell you something?"

Kiley nodded.

"If you repeat this I'll deny I ever said it," Susan began. "But . . . I actually think that, in some ways, the kids were better off with my sister. I know she can be crazy and . . . erratic. But I also know she really loves her kids. And she lets them *be* kids."

How could it be, Kiley wondered, that Susan and Platinum were sisters? Susan was so passive and Platinum was so . . . not. Kiley couldn't say she was fond of either of their personal styles, but if she had to choose one? Well, she'd choose Platinum. Minus the drugs and alcohol.

Judge Terhune rapped his gavel and asked for a half hour recess. He wanted to see all the lawyers in chambers. Susan skittered off to find her husband, snaking her way through the crowd. As Kiley waited patiently to get out the rear doors, she felt a hand on her elbow and heard a familiar slimy voice behind her.

"Hi, Kiley. How are you today?"

It was Spencer Lacroix, the tabloid editor. He wore a black suit with a white T-shirt underneath, and shades. Kiley hated people affected enough to wear sunglasses inside.

"I'm fine," Kiley replied, moving forward with the crowd.

Lacroix leaned close, breathing on Kiley in a way that she found repulsive, but clearly he didn't want to be overheard.

"Have you got an answer for me?" he asked. "You ready for a sit-down on your boss for big bucks?"

Kiley was jostled by a woman's oversized purse. She leaned as far away from Lacroix as she could.

"Our cover story's almost complete," he went on. "We just need a little inside information." He flashed a copy-paper-white smile. "The truth, baby, and nothing but."

Right there in the corridor, with people streaming past them on both sides, Kiley made her final decision.

"I don't want anything to do with you or your sleazy magazine." She made a beeline for the elevator, but Spencer kept up with her, weaving through the crowd.

"Maybe you'll change your mind when you hear about the new feature I have planned anyway, all about a virginal little good-girl nanny for Platinum who got her job via a reality show that tanked. She's come a long way from her childhood with an alcoholic father and a loony mother. How she hooked up with her supermodel boyfriend—we're still working on that angle."

Kiley swallowed hard. FAMOUS MODEL HAS AU PAIR GIRLFRIEND WITH THUNDER THIGHS. The *Universe* had probably already gotten close-up photos of her with a telescopic lens, pictures in which her upper legs would look like cottage cheese even without Photoshop. But that was nothing compared to having this slimeball write about her parents. That was *private*. She was a *private person*. How dare he threaten to write about her family?

Kiley knew instinctively not to let Lacroix see that he was getting to her. Willing herself to project cool, collected energy, she shrugged. "A story about me won't sell any papers."

He grinned, that too-familiar glint in his dark eyes. Not exactly the response she'd been hoping for. "Think it over, kiddo.

You talk to me about Platinum, and I'll kill my exposé on your little dysfunctional house on the prairie. Meantime, be sure not to miss our next issue. I think you'll find it *very* interesting." He spun on the heel of his Prada loafer, pulled his phone from his pocket, and headed in the opposite direction.

Kiley felt like throwing up. What if he really did write about her family? Her father would probably lose his job. And her mother . . . she would be so hurt. After giving Kiley permission to stay in Los Angeles as an emancipated minor. After giving Kiley her wings. *This* was how she would be repaid?

She needed advice from someone who would know how to handle this. She took out her cell phone and pressed in a familiar number.

10

"And then after he threatened me in person, this . . . this *cretin*, Spencer Lacroix, calls my cell *and* says not only is he going to write about me and my parents in the *Universe,* he's going to send copies to every corner of my extended family free of charge. They'll freak and I'll be on the next Greyhound to Wisconsin."

"Lordy," Lydia commented. She leaned back in the Horchow mahogany rocking chair and gazed up at the starry night sky. She and Kiley were in the backyard of the moms' estate—actually, Kat's estate now that Anya had departed. The exterior lights had been turned off; all that illuminated their faces was the cool blue light emanating from the bottom of the swimming pool. Inside, Martina and Jimmy were playing with their Wii (something they were allowed to do now that Anya was gone), every so often letting out squeals of excitement, while Kat was doing more prep work for the U.S. Open. When Lydia last saw her, she'd been watching videotapes of all of Serena Williams's matches for the last year, intensely charting her particular tendencies on the court.

Now that Anya was gone, things were different. The house no longer felt like a gulag. The kids actually relaxed. But sometimes Lydia would catch the sadness in their eyes. Kids always got the raw end of things when it came to divorce. Kat seemed melancholy, too. She and Anya had been together for eleven years. They had two children. It had to be horrible. Lydia hoped that time would heal her aunt's wounds. If not, she had some amazing powder she'd brought back from Amazonia that would make her feel like doing the hula on a tabletop. But that didn't seem exactly appropriate to offer for the time being.

And now here was Kiley, bringing a whole set of problems of her own. "Don't worry about the *Universe,*" she assured her friend. "This Lacroix dude is a jackass."

"All the more reason I should worry," Kiley shot back.

Good point. "Any chance your family will think it's a big ol' laugh riot to have a feature spot in the supermarket checkout aisle?"

Kiley gave her a baleful look. "Have you *met* my mom?"

Well, no, Lydia thought. They had never actually met. But Lydia clearly remembered seeing Mrs. McCann at the filming of *Platinum Nanny* at the Brentwood Hills Country Club pool. It was the same day Lydia first met Kiley. Her mother had been a nervous woman. Very nervous. Not the kind of person who would take well to a tabloid exposé.

"Remember when those producers forced your mom to wear that hat? And it was so god-awful orange that she looked like a polka-dotted highway crew leader?"

Kiley grimaced. "I was trying to forget that."

"My point is, your mom was embarrassed, but she sucked it up and so did you. If your mom was willing to wear that hat for you, then a dumb tabloid story should be a breeze. Your problem is that you let that tabloid guy get in your head. Now what you need to do is use it to your advantage."

"And how, pray tell, does one use her own dirt as an advantage?" Kiley knit her dark eyebrows, which, Lydia noted, were seriously in need of grooming.

"You know MySpace?"

Kiley laughed. "Only you would ask somebody that question. You were in the jungle too long. *Everyone* knows MySpace."

Lydia had brought out a pitcher of fresh juice, a blend of ten tropical fruits the cook had concocted. She poured some into one of the cocktail glasses that rested on a small glass-topped table nearby, then drank with satisfaction. "People put embarrassing crap about themselves on there all the time. It's like an Ama pissing contest. They actually have those, by the way. They're pretty cool. You would not believe how far some little five-foot-nothing guy can piss—"

"Lydia?"

"Hmmm?"

"Your mind is a scary place. Could you stick to the topic?"

"Point is, thanks to that dickhead Spencer, you can be famous. Famous is good. You wanted to be famous on *Platinum Nanny*."

"No, I didn't. I only did the show because it would mean I could stay in California and declare residency. And I only did that so I could get in-state tuition at Scripps after I graduate."

Lydia waved a hand dismissively. "Details. The point is, you were not afraid then and I see no need for you to be afraid now."

She sipped the juice and watched a shooting star flit across the sky.

"I guess." Kiley didn't sound convinced.

"It's survival of the toughest, sugar plum," Lydia said. "And frankly, you and your family are just not that fascinating to all of America. So don't let him work his mind games on you."

Before Kiley could answer, her cell chimed with the three preprogrammed notes that indicated a text message. She grumbled as she read it. "Gotta go. The colonel beckons. Don't get up, I know the way out."

Lydia stood anyway and walked her friend to the cement stairs leading up to the main house. Then she went back to the pool. She was too lazy to go get a bathing suit and it just so happened that she wasn't wearing any underwear. So she simply slipped out of her cutoffs and T-shirt and dove in. The water was magnificent, the same temperature as the air, and she swam a half mile easily.

When she climbed out and toweled off, her stomach grumbled. That hadn't changed from Amazonia. Swimming always gave her an appetite. She pulled on the same clothes she'd been wearing, then padded up to the main house to find something delicious. She went in through the back door.

Nothing could have prepared her for who she saw in the living room, sitting on the buttery Italian leather sofa next to her aunt.

It was her mother arrived, unannounced, from the Amazon.

Lydia raced for her mom's arms. Karen Chandler hugged her daughter, looking as if she could have stepped directly from the jungle. She wore bush shorts and a T-shirt advertising Coke—

her mother never paid any attention to what she wore. Her thick blond hair was frizzing out of a messy ponytail. Lydia didn't think she'd ever seen anyone so beautiful in her life.

"Mom!"

"Hi, sweetie."

"Oh Mom," Lydia murmured. "This is the best surprise."

Karen smiled. "I got a FedEx from Kat."

"FedEx? When did FedEx start delivering up the river?" Lydia was shocked. This would change life in the Amazon completely.

"About a week after you left, actually. They run a boat three times a week from Manaus. Costs a fortune. But I think they're using it in an advertisement."

"I know it was selfish of me," Kat said. She looked pale. There were dark circles under her eyes.

"Hey, I'm glad my little sister still needs me sometimes," Karen said.

Looking at them sitting together, it was so obvious they were related. They shared the same eyes, same hair. Even their body frames were near identical.

"How long will you be here?" Lydia was still in a state of shock.

Her mother shrugged. "As long as I need to be."

Kat smiled gratefully. "Take your mom upstairs to the green bedroom, okay? It's got the best shower. Eight showerheads."

"Heavenly." Karen sighed. "I'll just take a shower and then come back down, okay?"

Kat nodded. She already seemed lost in thought.

Lydia led her mother down the hallway. "Won't Dad need an

assistant?" She grabbed her mom's bag—a single dusty, battered canvas backpack.

"You remember Dr. Butkowski, don't you?"

How could Lydia forget? Right before she left, he was the well-meaning doctor whose introduction to the world of tribal medicine via a time-honored Amarakaire scrotum-cupping exchange probably left him permanently sissified.

"He came back," Karen explained. "He's working with your father now."

"Him?" Lydia was shocked. "Boy, I would've bet big bucks that he'd go running back to civilization faster than an Ama covered with honey when the black flies hatch."

Her mother laughed as they made their way up the grand staircase. "You never know."

Lydia gave her mother a quick version of the grand tour. The last time Karen had been in Los Angeles, Kat and Anya had lived in a different house, so this was entirely new to her. The kitchen, the sunroom, the game room, the sitting room, the indoor/outdoor back porch, the TV and media room, the family room, the formal living room, the formal dining room—all of it drew appropriate oohs and aahs from her mother. But her mom was most impressed by the library, where Anya kept her rare Russian novels, and where Lydia's hand trailed over a signed first edition of Dostoyevsky's *The Idiot*.

Her mother rubbed a forefinger along the book's spine. "This is so hard on Kat. She and Anya have been together forever."

"Between you and me, Mom? I can't stand the bitch." She led her mother down the hall to the green guest room.

"I couldn't stand her either, sweet pea," her mom confessed, falling back into her southern drawl as easily as Lydia had. "Every time Kat talked to me, I knew she wasn't really happy. She was like a serf in her own house, which is a bunch of heavy-handed, draconian horse dooky. I hope you're being treated better than that."

"Now that she's gone, and you're here . . . ?" Lydia smiled as she set her mom's bag on the floor next to the forest green quilt-covered king-sized bed. "Enjoy your shower. There's endless hot water. Stay in as long as you like."

"Where are you going?" Karen asked.

"My guesthouse."

"Good. I'll stop by after my shower. I want to hear every-thing. Where you eat, who your friends are, what your new school will be like . . . and most importantly, who's this boy Billy you wrote to me about."

Lydia started back to her guesthouse, but before she was out the back door of the main house she heard the main landline ring. Thinking that it might be Anya, and deciding she wanted to shield her aunt from talking to the Merry Matron of Moscow, she answered it in the kitchen. "Carpenter residence," Lydia chimed in a Scottish accent, having some fun at Anya's ex-pense. " 'Ooh are ya this evening?"

"Lydia? Is that you? Man, I lucked out. Can you speak up? I can't hear you very well."

Shit. The connection *was* bad, but there was no doubt about the voice. Luis Amador, the golf pro by day, stalker-freak by night, one-night-fling from hell.

"Luis? Why are you—how many times do I have to tell you? Just. Go. Away!"

The shaky phone line made the chuckling faint, but it was still there. "And how many times do I have to tell you? I am always here for you. Particularly now, since you broke up with your boyfriend and need a shoulder to cry on. Or a lap to sit on. Or a—"

Lydia cringed, her knuckles turning white around the neck of the handset. What was wrong with this guy?

"It's a real sad thing when a boy cannot take no for an answer," Lydia seethed. "Someone might think you're compensating for being on the small side. And I'm *not* talking about your height."

Luis laughed. "We both know that isn't true."

Shit. She didn't remember *anything* from that night, so she'd have to take his word for it. Another tack was called for. "Billy and I are exclusive now," she told him. "You and I had fun. But it's time to go have fun with some other lucky lady."

"Wait. You're still going out with him?" Luis sounded stunned.

"Right," Lydia confirmed. "So even *if* we slept together—and considering that I was too drunk to remember, which by the way, is an incredibly stupid thing to do that won't happen twice, thank you very much—the important thing is that Billy believes me. And you will never convince him otherwise."

"Well, you might think so, bitch. You might think you're done with the past, but you know what? The past isn't done with—"

Lydia couldn't take another moment of this. She slammed the phone down, then took the receiver off the hook in case Luis planned to call back. She'd hang it back up later.

What a scumbucket he had turned out to be! If he thought he was going to intimidate her, he was messing with the wrong trained-by-a-shaman girl.

11

With a crack that sounded around the stadium, the referee's assistant fired the starter's pistol to end the first half. Both teams—Bel Air High School in its blue uniforms with white letters, and Echo Park in its white unis with green and gold trim—straggled off the field as the public-address announcer declared the score.

"And at the end of the first half, the score is, the Echo Park Eagles, twenty-seven, and the Bel Air Bengals, three. Please welcome the Echo Park Eagles marching band to the field!"

"Olé, olé olé olé!" The cheer went up from the Echo Park bleachers. This cheer was so familiar to Esme; they always greeted the marching band with this Spanish chant taken from the world of soccer. The utterly bizarre thing was, she was not sitting with them.

Esme was sitting with the enemy.

How many times had she looked disdainfully over at the rich

kids from the rich school and hated them, with their salon-streaked hair and their designer whatever. Their Beemers and Jeeps and hot-shit little sports cars filled the parking lot. You knew which vehicles belonged to kids from Echo Park. The rusty pickup trucks. The pimp-your-ride vans with the oversized wheels and the ghetto-blasters. And then there was the way the rich kids would look at the Echo Park kids, like they smelled bad. It had pissed Esme off so much that she'd stopped going to away games.

Only now here she was. Part of *them*.

She'd arrived with Kiley and Lydia. Kiley had driven them in Platinum's white BMW 321i, and parked in the three-level parking structure north of the athletic complex. They paid the nominal admission charge and entered the vast, gleaming football stadium right out of *Remember the Titans*. Esme saw three or four girls she knew from the Echo. They cut their eyes at her; twitched their hips and whispered to one another, obviously about her. Esme told herself she didn't care—it wasn't as if she'd liked those girls when she was still in the Echo. Two of the girls, Consuela and Daisy, were in the Razor Girls and could gangbang with the best of 'em. In tenth grade, Daisy had a baby who was being raised by her mother. Consuela was in and out of juvie. Still, Esme couldn't help it. As she climbed the bleachers on the Bel Air side with Lydia and Kiley, she felt like a traitor.

Now it was halftime, and as much as she liked Lydia and Kiley, she really could not sit on the side where she did not belong another minute, even if she did go to school there. She excused herself and went around to the Echo side of the stadium, peering around, looking for her best friend, Jorge. He'd sent her a text message that he was coming to the game, but she hadn't seen him.

She slid into a seat next to Marisol, a shy girl with a long braid down her back who Esme knew from her honors English class. Marisol was also a friend of Jorge's.

"*¿Qué pasa, chica?*" Esme asked, falling into the cadence of the Echo without even thinking about it.

Marisol eyed her coolly. "Esme."

Marisol's friend Antoinette studied Esme through half-closed eyes. These girls were at the top of their class, two of the few Esme knew who would go on to college. And they didn't seem to like Esme any more than the gangbangers did.

"Have you seen Jorge?" Esme asked.

Marisol just shrugged. She two-fingered a homemade tostada from some aluminum foil and took a bite. Esme's mouth watered. Evidently Marisol had brought food made by her mother, who had a job in Santa Monica cooking for a famous movie director and his actress wife. A real job, because she'd actually been born in the United States; not an off-the-books-because-she-was-illegal job.

"How you like Gringo-land?" Antoniette asked.

How *did* she like it? How could she explain that it was wonderful and horrible at the same time? Over here the people looked like her. Dressed like her. Talked like her. Over here, she didn't have to feel strange about using Spanglish if she wanted, or even a word in Spanish if the Spanish word was better than an English one.

"It's okay" was all she finally said.

The Echo Park cheerleaders finished their cheer. Across the stadium, the Bel Air kids rose and cheered as one: "That's all right, that's okay, you're gonna work for us someday! That's all right, that's okay, you're gonna work for us someday!"

"Charming," came a familiar male voice that Esme would have known anywhere. She looked up. Jorge was standing in the aisle regarding her. "You slumming it?" he added.

She took in his familiar lanky frame and piercing dark eyes. Just seeing him made something inside her relax. He was the smartest person she knew; a poet, a rapper, a political organizer. Plus, he knew her better than anyone else in the world.

Jorge wore black jeans and a blue T-shirt. His hair had grown since Esme had last seen him, and he had it slicked back on his head. Not nearly as tall as Jonathan, nor as well built, but he was still very handsome. In fact, Esme thought he'd never looked better.

"Makes me not want to sit over there. Ever." Esme's eyes were dark.

"You really wanna define yourself by where you sit?" Jorge asked.

Esme shrugged. "Why not? Other people do."

"Oh, well then," Jorge mocked, a smile tugging at his lips.

Just looking at him made her realize how ridiculous she sounded. She watched the Echo Park band step onto the field wearing their familiar green and gold uniforms.

"So." Jorge shoved his hands into the pockets of his jeans. "You don't call, you don't write," he teased.

"I've been busy," Esme said.

"Jonathan?"

"Work," Esme replied. She didn't really like talking with Jorge about her love life. He hadn't approved of Junior, her former boyfriend. And she was sure he wasn't high on Jonathan, either.

"And soon school," he added. He tugged her away from

Marisol and Antoinette, who were listening in on their conversation while pretending not to. "Your parents are right, you know. This is a huge opportunity for you. Don't blow it."

"I don't need a third parent," Esme said crossly, tossing her hair off her face.

"Good, because I'm not in the market for a daughter," Jorge shot back. "The whole teen-dad thing is highly overrated."

"No shit," Esme agreed. She knew many teen dads, the vast majority of whom did not parent their kids. It always came down to the mom, age sixteen, fifteen, even fourteen, often with the help of her mom or grandparents. That, along with gang-banging, was the life Esme vowed she would never live.

The band started a medley of songs by Ricky Martin; Esme pretended to listen. But really, she was lost in thought. There'd been many strange experiences since she'd decided to come to live at the Goldhagens' and take care of their children. But this football game, where her old high school was playing her new high school, and where her old friends were sitting together on one side of the field, while the kids from her new school were on the other side of the field, had to be one of the strangest.

"I should go back over there," Esme mumbled. She was trying to pick out Lydia and Kiley from clear across the field but couldn't.

"Come on, Esme," Marisol called. "Be with your homegirls."

Oh. Great. *Now* they were her homegirls. Just a moment earlier they had been treating her like a traitor to La Raza.

"Now they're your homegirls, huh?" Jorge asked, his voice low, as if reading Esme's mind. But that was how it had always been with them. His eyes flicked over her. "You look nice," he added.

She was wearing a short black skirt and sandals with a skinny three-inch heel, and a black halter top. She sat with Jorge and they talked about everything, paying little attention to the game down below—Echo Park was way ahead. Jorge's band, the Latin Kings (he wrote the lyrics for their songs), had played at a recent immigration rally. He was already thinking about where he wanted to go to college and had recently been on a trip to Princeton with his parents to check it out. Esme knew he had the grades and the test scores to get in.

"You want to go to Princeton?" Esme asked. "Could you pick any place whiter?"

"Well, just think," Jorge teased, "I can rep all the brown people." He leaned his forearms on his thighs, hands dangling. "I don't know where I want to go yet, really. What about you?"

"I can't think past senior year of high school."

"Don't give me that," Jorge said sharply. "You *are* going to college."

"Fine, I'm going to college, I just don't want to talk about it."

Down on the field, the Echo Park marching band finished up its halftime show with the school fight song, and then marched off the field to thunderous whoops and hollers from the local fans. The announcer came on to say that in keeping with tradition, there was no Bel Air High School marching band, but that a famous BAHS graduate would be entertaining. The Bel Air side cheered when a former member of the Eagles was rolled out onto the field on the back of a flatbed truck with his band, and launched into "Hotel California."

Jorge stood up. "Your friends are here, right?"

Esme nodded.

"Then let's go over and say hi. I haven't seen Kiley in forever.

'Cept on television, of course." He laughed; so did Esme. Today's testimony at Platinum's trial had been all over the news, as a representative of the Los Angeles Police Department testified to the drugs that they'd found in Platinum's living room. Platinum's lawyer tried to argue that the drugs might have been planted, but Judge Terhune had disallowed the line of inquiry.

Esme hesitated. Across the way were Kiley and Lydia, yes. But there were all those other people. . . .

"I don't know, Jorge. Maybe we should just stay here and hang out."

"What? Eh, you afraid?" Jorge looked at her closely. "You can't be afraid. That's where you're going to be going to school. You made that decision already."

Esme fidgeted, and Jorge sat back down.

"I'm not like you," she told him.

"Not like me how? You're much better looking, not to mention just as smart and just as talented. Okay. You don't rap. But you're an artist, Esme."

"I don't get it," Esme ruminated. "Back in June, you were wondering if I should even take this job, or go to this school. Now, it's like you want me to be one of them. Jorge, I'll never *be* one of them."

Jorge grinned. "Now, my girl is being honest. Tell me what you're thinking."

Through the rest of halftime, and most of the third quarter, Esme talked and Jorge listened. All the time they'd grown up together in the Echo, she'd felt that Jorge was like a brother to her—a wiser, smarter brother, even though they were the same age. Jorge's father was a public defender. Jorge himself talked about going to law school at UCLA, working in government, and running for mayor. It wasn't impossible. The current mayor was Latino. All it took was brains and drive, and Jorge had plenty of both.

Esme told him about Tarshea. About Jonathan. About what was going on with her tattoo business and how much money she was making. About the weird orientation sessions she'd had here at this very school. About how the hopes and dreams of June had come crashing into the hard reality of August. About how she was having second thoughts about anything and everything.

"You finished?"

Esme nodded, and she felt Jorge's muscular arm go around her. It was the nicest gesture that he could make, and she felt so comfortable.

"You have a lot going on," he acknowledged. Then he stood and reached a hand down to her. "I'm gonna mull all that. We'll talk about it later. Now let's go say hi to your friends."

His arm stayed around her all the way down the bleachers, and all the way around the field.

She spotted Kiley first, about halfway up the bleachers on the Bel Air side. With the score sitting at forty-five to ten, and only ten minutes to go in the game, the crowd had thinned out considerably. Also sitting with Kiley and Lydia were two of the girls who'd given them the orientation tour. Staci what's-her-name and Amber. Staci wore an aqua-and-brown-polka-dotted babydoll tunic with brown leggings and ballet flats. Amber wore a lace kimono over skinny jeans and sky-high Jimmy Choos. They had guys with them—cute in a generic, we're-cool-rich-boys kind of way.

"Hey, y'all!" Lydia called when she saw them. "Were you guys across the field hollerin' for the other team?"

"Yeah," Esme said, just as Echo Park scored another touchdown.

"Evidently it worked," Jorge added with a laugh.

Staci and Amber had to wait patiently to be introduced. Then they introduced the guys. Richie, the red-haired guy, was Staci's boyfriend, and was in the film program at USC. Trent was with Amber—he went to BAHS, and Amber reported that he played guitar in a fast-rising post-punk group that already had gigs at some of the biggest clubs in Hollywood.

"And how do you know Jorge?" Staci asked easily.

Here it was. Esme was going to have to admit the truth. That she knew him from the Echo. Then there'd have to be a long explanation of who Jorge wasn't. That he wasn't a gangbanger. That he wasn't a hood. That he wasn't going to take names and numbers and come back with his *cholos*.

No, wait. She didn't owe them any explanations. She didn't have to tell them shit. Before Esme could decide what to do, Jorge did it for her. And he did it in such a funny, charming, disarming way that Staci and Amber were utterly dazzled.

"Your friend is so cool!" Staci exclaimed. "You've got to come out with us sometime and party, Jorge. Did I pronounce your name correctly? I took three years of Spanish." She batted her perfectly mascaraed eyes at him. Esme suspected instantly that she had extensions glued on.

"You said it perfectly," Jorge assured her.

"We're just thrilled that we've got Esme and her friends in our class this year," Amber said. "It's always so boring, same people, same faces. And even the new faces are the same. Just like ours. But these girls?" Amber indicated Kiley, Esme, and Lydia. "These girls are a breath of fresh air."

"They're so fun. We're gonna hang out together and party and everything." Then Staci looked at her watch with regret.

"Well, I guess we're gonna book. Trent's playing a gig at a private party in Mar Vista tonight. Wish we could invite you guys, but you know how it is."

"Have fun," Lydia told them.

After a round of warm goodbyes, Staci and Amber took off with their boyfriends.

"See? Not so bad," Jorge told Esme.

"Please. That was as much of a game as the one that just got played down there." Kiley chucked her chin toward the field, where the gun had just gone off to end the game. Echo Park had killed—fifty-one to ten. There was only the most cursory of postgame handshaking on the field.

"Jorge, Bel Air girls are not your strong suit. The fact is, they hate us," Esme explained. "Well, me and Kiley, anyway. They think Lydia is cool."

Esme looked at her friend from the Echo. He seemed truly surprised.

"Don't you get it?" Esme asked Jorge, irritated at his innocence. "They were playing us!" Something hard and hot turned in her stomach. Her fingers balled into fists. She wasn't a violent person, but she would have liked to hurt those girls, because she knew what Jorge didn't seem to comprehend.

"You know that expression 'kill 'em with kindness'?" she asked Jorge.

He nodded.

"Bang-bang. We're dead."

12

"Hurry up, y'all. I *knew* we should have come earlier."

Lydia was practically dragging Martina and Jimmy by their wrists through the booths and tents that comprised the Melrose Trading Post, lamenting the fact that these booths were closing almost as fast as she passed them.

That's what I get for showing up at four o'clock, Lydia thought.

The chichi flea market in the midst of the Fairfax district—a Los Angeles neighborhood that was equal parts hipster and Orthodox Jews—had bloomed from the attention of Hollywood stars and the bargain-savvy alike. Here, on the torrid asphalt of the parking lot at Fairfax High School, would-be Melrose Avenue merchants and flea marketers met to sell their wares.

The assortment of stuff available was staggering, as was the crowd that came from all over the city. One-of-a-kind designer clothes and furniture hid in plain sight alongside random junk. On previous outings to the flea market, Lydia had scored a vintage hot pink silk Chanel bed jacket and a tweed Dior pencil skirt (the lining was ripped, but so what?). She'd also scored a Nanette Lepore leopard-print chiffon blouse (missing buttons, which was why it was selling for eight bucks, when Lydia knew for a fact that at Neiman Marcus a similar shirt *with* the buttons was currently going for north of three hundred dollars). She'd found it crumpled up between an empty propane tank and a rusting saxophone.

If you had taste and a good eye, the place was a fashion gold mine.

"Come on, come on," Lydia insisted.

"It's too hot to walk fast," Jimmy whined.

Martina yanked away from her. "No! We're leaving Faith behind."

That's right. Faith. Kat had taken Lydia's mom to Valerie's on Rodeo Drive for an eyebrow waxing, and Lydia had brought Martina and—wonder of wonders—a *friend of Martina's* to the flea market. Lydia had never known her cousin to have a friend before, so she considered this a wonderful sign. That friend, Faith, was now twenty yards back. She was lost in a world of her own, adjusting her glasses and hovering over a table attended by a cadaverous guy dressed in black with a beard nearly to his navel. That table, Lydia saw, was littered with nothing but junk: a neon beer sign, an assortment of lampshades, and what looked to be a carved wooden pterodactyl.

On one hand, Lydia was thrilled for Martina. Her cousin had met Faith Phillips, whose father, Bingham Phillips, was executive producer of a very popular reality show, at the country club. On the other hand, the friend was Faith. With her two-hundred-dollar streaked chestnut brown hair and disdainful dark eyes, haughty Faith treated Lydia like an unwanted escort for the day. She was a year older than Martina, and thought she knew better about everything. On the ride here from her home in Pacific Palisades—X detoured there to pick her up—Faith had issued long dictates concerning everything related to taste: the best food (soy curd), acceptable clothing (FUBU was in, Juicy Couture was out), music (ABA—Anyone but Avril), and the funniest movie star (Adam Sandler, not Ben Stiller).

"You just ditched my friend!" Martina cried, and stomped back to Faith. Lydia followed. Jimmy groaned, folded his arms, and refused to budge.

"Wait right there!" Lydia called to him. Faith was examining a crystal pin in the shape of a dolphin. "Faith, honey, try to keep up, okay?"

Faith ignored Lydia and held the pin up for Martina to examine. "Do you like it?"

"Do you?" Martina asked, afraid to venture an opinion lest Faith disagree.

"Dolphins are out," Faith pronounced, tossing the jewelry back into a tray crowded with cheap trinkets. "Unicorns are in."

"This is so boring!" Jimmy yelled, marching over to them.

"We can look for things you like," Lydia offered.

He folded his arms. "I don't like *anything*."

It wasn't really like Jimmy to be so negative. Now that Lydia thought about it, he'd hardly said anything all day, except for occasionally complaining. From the moment Faith had gotten in the car, he'd been silent. He hadn't talked about any of his favorite subjects—bugs, golf, or the Dodgers.

"You want to see if we can find you a new Dodgers cap?" Lydia offered.

Jimmy shook his head and stared at the ground.

"The Dodgers are out. The Mets are in," Faith pronounced.

Lydia sighed. It had been a mistake to bring Jimmy on a shopping expedition. She craned her neck longingly and peered at the stands where hidden couture treasures awaited her. "How about if you let us three girls shop for clothes and stuff for just a half hour," Lydia decreed, "and after that we'll do whatever you want."

"I don't care." He turned away from her.

"All the clothes they have here are crap," Faith said.

"Right," echoed Martina.

This untruth was nearly enough to make Lydia weep. And yet here was Martina buying right into it.

"Y'all, follow me," Lydia said, and made a beeline for a booth where she'd found treasures in the past. She pawed through a row of skirts until she came to a darling yellow eyelet number going for the delightful sum of seven bucks; Lydia noted that it was a Chloé with the tag ripped out.

"This skirt at Saks would sell for hundreds," Lydia explained, holding it up to Martina. "It's an amazing bargain!"

"No offense, but you only think that because you have bad taste," Faith said. "If it was worth so much money, it wouldn't be here. I'm thirsty, can we get something to drink? Not Fiji water. Fiji water is out. Smart Water is in."

"I'm thirsty, too," Martina said.

Sigh. Lydia made a mental vow never to bring the children here again. She found the nearest refreshment stand and bought them all soft drinks and french fries, which she figured would keep them happy for the next fifteen minutes.

The girls chowed down, but Jimmy ignored what Lydia knew

to be his favorite food. He wandered over to a display of small toys and began twirling a Rubik's Cube. Lydia dimly remembered having one in Texas before she'd been dragged off to Ama country. It was a box with six different colors on it. The object was to keep turning the colors until one side was solid blue, one red, one yellow, one orange, one white, and one green.

Impulsively, Lydia called out to the shopkeeper, who was an elderly lady in a flowered dress. "How much for the Rubik's Cube?"

The woman held up five laconic fingers.

"Dollars?"

"No, euros. Of course dollars," the woman said. She had a strong Russian accent that immediately reminded Lydia of Anya. "You want?"

Jimmy tossed the cube back onto the table. "No." He walked away.

Yep. There was definitely something wrong. Lydia chalked it up to the disruption of Anya leaving home. She caught up with Jimmy. "You're feeling kinda punky, huh?"

"What do you care?" Jimmy sneered.

Wow. He really was taking the moms' breakup hard. Lydia decided she'd talk to Kat about it. She bought them all soft-serve ice cream—at least Jimmy ate that—and then called X to come pick them up.

On the way home, Jimmy didn't say one word at all.

Seven hours after leaving the flea market—midnight, to be exact—Lydia was winding her way through the dense, sweaty crowd at Surf's Up, a new club on the beach in Venice. X had dropped her on the way to some place he wanted to visit in

Marina del Rey, with the promise that he'd pick her up later if she needed a ride. She'd asked Billy if he wanted to join her, but he had begged off. He was doing set decoration for a music video that was being shot on a yacht, and he couldn't get out of the gig even if he'd wanted to.

That was fine. Lydia liked going out by herself. In fact, the night she'd met Billy, she had been out at a club alone. And this one, with its pounding surf-punk music, surfboard theme, and buff waiters in jam shorts and nothing else, was very appealing. It was apparently appealing to hundreds of others, as there'd been a line outside that stretched for fifty yards down the beach. That hadn't stopped Lydia, though. Wearing a sheer green slip dress over a lacy black bra had been a wise choice. The behemoth of a door guy had given her a quick once-over, then waved her inside. No cover charge, either.

Lydia stood in the center of the throng and exulted. The bass thumped, half-naked bodies grinded—the club encouraged people to shed their tops (there was the moral equivalent of a coat check just for shirts, and if you went barechested you got a coupon for two-for-one drinks)—and Smart Lights reacted synchronously with the music, changing color, focus, and diffusion. This was perfect. She didn't want to think. She didn't want to yack. All she wanted to do was dance.

She moved onto the dance floor and started to sway to the music.

"Hey, Lydia! You found us!" Staci waved her arms. "Look, you guys. It's Lydia!"

A moment later, the trio besieged her and was pulling her toward the bar, offering to buy her a drink—any drink.

Lydia was conflicted. Yes, Staci had called her earlier to

suggest she come to this club. And yes, she'd wanted to see it. But she felt guilty as hell being here without Kiley and Esme. She told herself that if she ran into the girls, she'd do her best to convince them how wrong they were about her friends. And if the girls continued to be assholes about it, she'd ditch them. Forever.

The bar area was packed. "I'd love a drink," Lydia said. "But I don't feel like waiting that long."

"We never wait," Amber said, tossing her head so that her dangling cherry-shaped rhinestone (or were they diamonds, Lydia wondered) earrings sparkled. She wore low-slung brown and aqua plaid Imitation of Christ trousers and a sheer aqua tank top, looking, Lydia thought, about as perfect as a girl could look.

If you liked that kind of thing.

Staci—dressed in a canary yellow Zac Posen babydoll with skinny jeans that Lydia had coveted at Fred Segal, merely raised her right hand toward the bar, waving two fingers with a come-hither look, and a bare-chested and goateed bartender appeared, smiling as if he had all the time in the world.

"Does everybody know what they want?" Staci asked.

"Flirtinis," Zona declared. "All around."

Staci nodded, and the bartender disappeared. "It's good publicity for their club when I show up," she explained to Lydia. "They think maybe my father will use this for a location in a movie. Guess who's here tonight?"

Lydia was usually pretty good at this game. When she'd lived in Amazonia, she devoured the magazines that were air-dropped in, or brought in by doctor and nurse volunteers. The interior of her mud hut had been decorated with celebrity photographs torn from these magazines. They didn't last long, of course. The humidity and the insects got to them quickly.

The bartender pushed four drinks across the metal bar, and Staci took hers. "Justin. See the guy with the big glasses, coat, and Italian hat?"

Lydia squinted. "You mean that guy?"

"That guy," Staci acknowledged. "Want to meet him?"

Lydia couldn't help herself. "I'd love to!"

This was fantastic. This was why she had come to L.A. It was as if she was being repaid with interest for all those months in the rain forest with an indigenous people whose idea of fun was to pierce their cheeks with sticks. Lydia had mixed feelings about her life in Amazonia. She'd learned a lot, and she'd lived in a way that few Americans ever could. But there were no clubs like Surf's Up on the Rio Negro.

"So, Lydia. Are you having a good time?" Staci's question was direct.

"Fab!" Lydia replied. She was not one to mute her enthusiasm.

"Good, because we've been talking." Staci traded a significant look with Amber and Zona, then turned back to Lydia. "We've decided we like you."

Only at this point did Amber and Zona smile. Phew.

Lydia smiled. "Great."

"But," Staci went on, "there is a little problem."

"It's about your friends," Amber added.

Big shocker. Well, Lydia was ready. But first, she wanted to hear all the ugly and despicable things these girls had to say. In all their glory.

"My friends?" Lydia echoed. She did everything but bat her

sooty lashes to emphasize her "innocence" at the query. "What about them?"

"We have a split decision on that girl Kiley," Staci explained. "Platinum's nanny. She might have possibilities, but she's got a lot of work to do."

Zona nodded emphatically. "Her clothes? Ohmigod, who dresses like that?"

"Plus she's a little fat," Amber went on. "Not, like, superhuge or anything. But really she could take off, like, ten pounds."

"Interesting," Lydia said. She knew exactly how to keep her face neutral so that these snotty girls had no clue what was really going on in her head.

"Okay, so anyway, Kiley is a maybe," Staci summed up. "But that chick Esme?" She rolled her eyes.

"I wore an outfit just like hers when we did *West Side Story* last year," Amber added maliciously. "She looks so cheap."

"By 'cheap' did you mean . . . *Latina*?" Lydia asked, smiling so that they'd think this was a friendly question.

"We are not racist," Zona insisted. "Jennifer Lopez's niece happens to go to our school. Her dad is a music producer. She lives in that redbrick mansion on Crest Hill."

"Esme comes from the Echo," Staci explained. "I mean, she was sitting with those gangbangers."

Lydia lifted one eyebrow. "She was sitting with her old friends. How do you know they're gangbangers?"

"Echo Park High is full of 'em," Staci said. "Everyone knows that. That is, for the kids that actually go to high school."

"Uh-huh," Lydia agreed. "But, see, I don't think that means that *everyone* in Echo Park is a banger. Any more than *everyone* in Bel Air is a snob."

Staci gave Lydia a cool look. "If it talks like a duck and walks like a duck . . ."

Her friends giggled.

"I know a gangbanger when I see one," Staci went on, flicking an imaginary speck of something off her shoulder. "Plus, I heard she does gang tattoos."

"Oh, y'all have that totally wrong," Lydia said. "She's a tattoo *artist*. She does freehand designs and charges a mint. She inks the biggest stars in Hollywood. I mean, she's booked up for like a year in advance."

This, Lydia knew, was perhaps a slight exaggeration. But it was worth it for a good cause—to get these girls to see the error of their preconceptions.

Amber narrowed her eyes. "Did you make that up or is it true?"

"Of course it's true," Lydia replied.

Staci shrugged. "All I know is what I heard. If I wanted to be friends with a girl and she had hideous accessories, I would be kind enough to tell her to lose the accessories. If I want to be friends with a girl and her hideous accessories are her other *friends* . . . then I tell her to lose the friends," she concluded.

Lydia nodded thoughtfully. "I sure do appreciate how you put that. Now I'm lookin' at it in a whole new light."

"We thought you would," Zona sniffed.

"You'll see," Amber added. "Being friends with us means your senior year will rock."

"I'm going to the ladies' room," Lydia said. "And while I'm gone, I'm going to give all this some serious thought. Y'all make some very good points."

Staci beamed and turned to her friends. "See? I told you she'd see it our way."

"Excuse me, y'all."

Lydia left the girls at the bar. She hoped they were still waiting a half hour later, when she was in the Audi with X and he was driving her home.

She might be from a place where women put plates in their ears and called it fashion, but she had her standards.

13

"You floated a mile high in the sky in a balloon with me. You can put your head underwater."

Tom's words made Kiley break out in a cold sweat, even though it was eighty-five degrees at ten o'clock on this sunny Sunday morning. They were at the adult pool at the country club, the colonel and his wife having taken Serenity and Sid to the PX at Edwards Air Force Base to buy them back-to-school clothes. The only reason that Kiley wasn't a part of the shopping excursion was that Serenity hadn't wanted Kiley to witness what she referred to as her "humiliation."

They were supposed to return to the Crossroads School in Santa Monica, one of the more liberal private schools in the city, but the colonel was making noises about sending Serenity and Sid to Father Ryan Elementary and Bruce to Father Ryan High School. Both these Catholic schools were renowned for their discipline. All three kids had already threatened to run away if this happened.

When Tom heard that Kiley had the morning free, he proposed this outing to the club so that they could take a whack—together—at Kiley's so-called anxiety attacks underwater. Tom hoped that if he was with Kiley, she'd be able to put her head underwater wearing scuba gear. And since he was a certified scuba diver himself—he'd learned on a modeling shoot at the Egyptian resort of Sharm El Sheikh—he was able to check out some gear from the recreation manager at the club.

It was a magnificent August day. Warm temperatures, blue skies, a gentle breeze, and a club that was mercifully empty of members this early in the day. But Kiley had so many things on her mind that it was tough for her to focus. Tomorrow, she'd be testifying at Platinum's trial. She hoped that the lawyers wouldn't grill her to death. Meanwhile, she'd been putting off calling her mother and father in Wisconsin to tell them about the upcoming article in the *Universe*. Mostly, she was starting to think that the editor she'd met outside the courthouse had been bluffing.

The alternative was too upsetting to contemplate. And then, there was the prospect of starting school in a couple of weeks having made exactly no new friends outside of Esme and Lydia. She wasn't all that sure that Esme would even be going to school.

She and Tom had talked about all of this on their way to the club, when they stopped at the Brentwood Coffee Bean for café Americanos and a couple of fresh-baked brioches. They'd stood in line behind Reese Witherspoon and Jake Gyllenhaal, and Tom had counseled that the best thing Kiley could do today was not worry about things over which she had no control.

"I wish we were back in Iowa, on my parents' farm," Tom had mused.

"How come?"

He got a mischievous glint in his eye. "We could bring slops out to the pigs. We've got a couple dozen. Pigs, slops—that grounds you in the reality of what you can control real fast."

Kiley had laughed, because she knew what he was talking about. She'd spent more than enough time on farms belonging to cousins and friends, though these tended to specialize in corn and dairy instead of soybeans and alfalfa like Tom's family. You could control bringing the slops to the pigs. What happened after that—how the pigs assaulted the trough—that was out of your hands.

"I think trying to go underwater in scuba gear will have the same operative effect," she noted.

"I know you can do this."

She'd pursed her lips skeptically. "I don't."

"Willing to try, that's all that matters."

Now, here they were, in water up to their chests in the pool. Tom had given her the pep talk, but Kiley's knees felt like jelly underwater. She couldn't help it; she remembered the awful feeling the last time she was in this pool with scuba gear. How she'd practically blacked out, how her heart had raced. How she was sure she had the same panic-disorder affliction as her mother. That disorder had ruined her mother's life. Kiley feared it could ruin her own. If she wasn't able to scuba dive, how could she ever be a marine biologist?

"My plan is to work off what you can do," Tom told her. He kept his voice low so that no one would overhear. "You're a good swimmer. You've had your head underwater thousands of times when you're swimming."

"That's a big duh."

"What I want to do is take it a step at a time. You've been underwater with a mask?"

"Yep."

"Then just put the mouthpiece in. Give me the mask."

Kiley frowned. "That doesn't make any sense."

"Hey. It can't hurt. What you tried before didn't work."

Tom put out his hand for the black mask that Kiley had pushed up to her hairline, and Kiley handed it over.

"Cool. Now, when you're ready, get your head wet . . . after you put the mouthpiece in," Tom instructed.

Kiley reached for the soft rubber mouthpiece and put it in her mouth. It tasted vaguely salty.

"You look like an alien," Tom cracked. Then, he pointed to the water. "Pretend you're a swimming alien."

Somehow, the idea of standing there with a rubber mouthpiece between her lips was more embarrassing than the idea of panicking underwater. Kiley let her knees bend and felt the water up to her neck. Over her mouthpiece. Over her head. Over her head. It was over her head. And she was *not* dying.

She popped up out of the water, spit out the mouthpiece, and grinned at Tom. "Did it."

"Halfway home. Now let's see you do it with the mask." He gave the mask to her. She slipped it on, ignoring the pain as it pulled at her now-wet hair. That got her thinking about her breathing. Yes, it was definitely shallower. And her heart. It was definitely starting to race.

"What—what makes you think it's going to be different?" Kiley managed.

Tom edged closer to her. "Because I'm here."

"So?" Kiley managed to gasp.

"So I'm not going to let anything happen to you. Kiley, look at me."

She looked at him through the glass of her face mask. He held her gaze for several seconds before he spoke again, and then only after he took both of her hands in his.

"You trust me?"

She nodded. But she wasn't convinced.

"Okay. On four, we're going under together," he instructed. "Everyone else does it on three. I figure three is never enough. Okay, one. Two. Three. And four."

He was holding her hands again, and she felt them tug her downward. She resisted for the briefest instant, then gave in, his words echoing in her mind: *I'm not going to let anything happen to you.*

And then, she was under, her eyes open, viewing the pool underwater with the rubber mouthpiece clenched between her teeth. He waved and smiled at her. She resisted the urge—God, it was so strong—to push off the rough pool bottom with her feet and rip the mouthpiece out of her mouth so that she could breathe the good air.

He grinned underwater, his eyes open. Then he gave her a thumbs-up and popped up out of the water. She took that as her signal to do the same, breaking the surface and spitting out the mouthpiece all in one motion. "I did it! I did it! I freaking did it!" she exulted, and pumped a fist in the air.

"You did." He held his arms wide, right there in the pool, and she moved into them for a long and delicious hug. There were more people in the pool now, mostly swimming laps, but no one was paying any attention.

"I don't understand, though. Why I couldn't do this myself." She clung to him, so grateful.

His arms tightened around her in the nicest way. "You'll do it alone next time. You just needed a better teacher. Now, you ready to breathe? It's easier than holding your breath."

Tom was right. Five minutes later, he had the regulator working, air flowing, and Kiley was sitting on the bottom of the pool, breathing. The possibilities made her feel drunk with happiness. She'd had to drop out of the scuba class earlier in the summer. Bruce had continued—she had to be a couple of weeks behind. But now that she could do it, maybe she could get the regular scuba instructor to get her caught up. Or maybe even Tom could teach her.

Tom had no idea the gift he'd just given her, Kiley decided. He'd given her back her future.

An hour later, they were together on the patio outside the clubhouse. The Sunday brunch at the country club was an extraordinarily lavish affair, even for a club whose combined membership income topped the gross national product of most Caribbean nations. The cooks had all donned white outfits and official blue Brentwood Hills Country Club toques, and were arrayed behind buffet tables that encircled the patio. Each Sunday had a theme, and this Sunday's was Mexico. Not only was there a mariachi band strolling from table to table, playing romantic songs, but there was also a margarita fountain. There weren't just the usual chimichangas, tortillas, and variations on carne asada, either. Every part and aspect of Mexican cuisine was represented, from the *chilaquiles* of Sinaloa to the *huilatotas* of Hidalgo. The aromas drifting over the patio were mesmerizing. Combined with the heady endorphin rush Kiley felt from having conquered the scuba gear, she was in a great place.

She and Tom had just come back from filling their plates to the white-tableclothed table for two when her cell rang. She answered automatically when she saw the number was blocked. "Kiley McCann."

"Kiley, this is Spencer Lacroix at the *Universe* with a quick courtesy message. The story about you and your family is running on Monday. Our corporate counsel is White and Rogerson in New York, should you need to contact them. The magazine will be on newsstands tomorrow at noon. I'm afraid you made the wrong decision, Kiley. The story would run with or without you. You made a poor choice. Literally. Goodbye."

"Wait!" Kiley cried.

It was too late. He'd hung up.

"You look like you've just been informed the police are coming for you," Tom observed.

"Almost as bad. It was the *Universe*. They're running the story. Tomorrow."

Tom grimaced. "It didn't go away, huh?"

"Not hardly. Damn!"

Kiley looked down at her brunch. The plate, filled with so many good things, had been alluring just a few moments ago. Now, she had zero appetite. She glanced at the tables around her. All of them were filled: laughing couples, families, golfers, tennis players, people drinking and eating and having fun. She recognized celebrities from TV and the movies. Some of them surely had to have been the subject of tabloid journalism. How did they feel when it happened?

"You'd better call your parents. Tell them what's coming. You want me to give you some privacy?"

"Stay," Kiley told him, putting her hand on his. "I've got it covered. I'm going inside. Back in a minute."

"I'll come with, if you want."

He was such a great guy! "Thanks," Kiley said. "But this one I have to tackle on my own."

She walked across the patio into the main clubhouse. Since so many of the members were part of the entertainment industry, the club had a private business center with soundproof cubicles. Each of the cubicles had a black leather easy chair, high-speed Internet hookup, cell-and-computer charging station, and a sleek gunmetal gray desk. At this time on a Sunday, the center was deserted. Still, she went into the most distant cubicle and closed the door. This phone call was going to suck.

Sunday morning. Her mother would be at the Derby, the restaurant where she waitressed. There'd be the usual post-church crowd, since it was the early afternoon in La Crosse. Hopefully, she'd have a little time to talk. Or maybe, hopefully she wouldn't. Kiley speed-dialed.

"Hello? Kiley? Is that you? Why are you calling on a Sunday afternoon? You don't usually call on a Sunday afternoon. You call on Sunday night!"

Yikes. Her mother sounded more anxious than usual. And that was saying a lot.

"I'm sorry, Mom. It's just that there's something I—"

"Hold on, Kiley. Hold on. I've got a table of seven on the warpath."

Kiley held. And held, and held. Five minutes. Ten minutes. Fifteen minutes. But her mother didn't come back. Kiley had been in the Derby so many times that she could picture the scene. Some family of seven badgering her mom because their burgers came out medium-well instead of medium, or because the short stack of pancakes wasn't short enough, or because they wanted their ranch dressing on the side of their house salad instead of on it. Her mother, queen of the overstressed, couldn't handle the questions. Her boss would have to step in. Thank God Jeanne McCann had worked at the Derby forever. The manager didn't have the heart to fire her.

Twenty minutes, though, was enough for Kiley. She clicked off. Her mother would call her back. She was sure of it.

14

Kiley slapped silent her blaring alarm clock, then burrowed under the sheets. Monday morning. Zero hour of what could possibly be the worst day of her life. Of course she had known this day was coming, but now that she was faced with the reality . . . testifying plus article in the *Universe* equaled disaster. No wonder a lump the size and feel of an overripe cantaloupe had settled in the pit of her stomach.

Ten minutes later, when she forced herself out from under the duvet and swung her feet onto the floor, she noticed that someone—probably the colonel, possibly one of the kids—had shoved the front section of the *Los Angeles Times* under her door. She shuffled over to pick it up, and gulped when she read the front-page headline: NANNY TO TESTIFY IN PLATINUM CUSTODY CASE; STORIES OF DRUG USE AND NEGLECT EXPECTED.

She frowned. Not that the headline was wrong, exactly. Kiley knew that she had to be honest about life with Platinum, as much as it would hurt to tell the jury about her former boss's addictions and alcoholism and absentee parenting. But there was no way around it. She would be under oath. One thing she would not do was lie in court.

The night before she'd laid out her clothes, in close consultation with Lydia. She'd decided to take the witness stand in a knee-length tartan Club Monaco skirt paired with a plain white button-down blouse. Lydia had found the skirt for Kiley marked down three times at Nordstrom, because there was a tiny fray in the hem.

She showered, dressed, put on the barest amount of mascara, lip gloss, and blush, and found herself the first one at breakfast in the main house. Breakfast was a lavish affair prepared by Mrs. Cleveland according to the colonel's orders: eggs, waffles, toast, hash browns, and coffee made with beans from the PX at Edwards Air Force Base. But she had no appetite; all she could handle was a slice of cantaloupe and black coffee. Mrs. Cleveland quietly wished her good luck testifying, then went into the pantry to get ready for the rest of the day's meals.

When Susan and the colonel entered, dressed in almost identical navy blue suits, the colonel cut right to the chase. "Kiley," he barked, which was a step up from "McCann," which was what he usually called her. "Where are the kids?"

"Still upstairs, I think."

"Breakfast is at 0800 hours. If they're not down here in ten minutes, they don't eat. I trust you're ready for your big day?"

"As much as I can be."

The colonel looked stern. "I will remind you that you will be promising on the Good Book to tell the truth. Now, we may have had our differences in the past, but I know you're a good girl, and I know you will take an oath like that seriously."

133

The colonel's pep talk—Kiley was stunned that he, of all people, was referencing the Bible—was cut off by Sid and Serenity. They careened into the room together, talking at once, competing for Kiley's attention.

"Kiley, you're gonna be on our side, right? I mean, you want Mom to come back home, don't you?" Serenity clutched Kiley's hand.

"You can't tell them the whole truth, Kiley," Sid added. "It'll ruin my mom, and she'll never be able to come home and we'll be living with Uncle Platoon forever!" He shot a look at the colonel, who glared back at him. "No offense, sir," he added with an eye roll.

"Where's your brother?" the colonel demanded.

"Upstairs. You want him, go get him," Serenity fired back.

Kiley put one hand on each kid's arm and fought to keep a smile off her face. The younger kids were regaining at least a little of their normal defiance. Kiley found it refreshing. "Believe me, I am not looking forward to this any more than you are. But I can't lie. I saw your mom doing drugs in this house, in front of you. Parents just can't do that. It's not legal, and it's not right."

"It's not like I ever noticed," protested Sid. "I mean okay, maybe she was using drugs, but it wasn't like I sat there and watched her. Maybe I *passed through* the room or something . . . but that's different. Right? Right?"

Two eager faces stared up at Kiley. Beneath their eagerness, Kiley saw something deeper. Something profound. There was real love and concern for their mother. It tore her up inside. The cantaloupe in her stomach morphed into a watermelon and started bouncing off her abdominal walls.

"Excuse me," she told everyone, and hurried from the kitchen.

"Where are you going, McCann?" the colonel boomed.

So she was back to being "McCann" again. "To be sick, sir," she called over her shoulder. "See you in the car."

Kiley had her right hand in the air.

"Miss McCann, do you promise to tell the truth, the whole truth, and nothing but the truth, so help you God?"

"I do." The bailiff backed away, and the lead prosecutor approached the witness stand as a murmur of anticipation ran through the jammed courtroom. People were anxious to hear what the nanny had to say. Kiley actually saw spectators leaning forward with anticipation. Then she saw Serenity, Bruce, and Sid sitting together, staring daggers at her. She felt sick all over again.

She'd been called as a hostile witness. That meant the prosecutor could ask her leading questions.

He bored right in with few preliminaries. "Miss McCann, you are employed by Platinum as her children's nanny, correct?"

Kiley nodded.

"Please answer yes or no."

"Yes," she managed.

"And you came to work for her through a television show, isn't that right?"

"Yes. I entered a reality-show contest called *Platinum Nanny,* and the prize was that the winner would move into Platinum's house and care for her kids," Kiley explained. Her mouth was so dry that her lips were sticking to her teeth. The show got canceled, but she hired me anyway."

"Very good. And I take it you were in her employ on the night of her arrest?"

"Yes." Again, Kiley nodded. She noticed a sketch artist in the gallery working away—probably a sketch of her, she realized. How weird was that? Straight ahead and a little to her right, Platinum sat ramrod straight next to her attorney at the defense table. Her signature hair was styled in a tidy chignon, and she eyed Kiley curiously, clearly unsure of what Kiley was about to say.

It was hard to focus, as the morning's events flooded back into her mind. Her arrival at the courthouse had been greeted by the biggest media circus yet. Tents had been set up—tents!—to shield multiple reporters and piles of camera equipment. Paparazzi lined a narrow walking tunnel flanked by police. Pro- and anti-Platinum supporters carried signs and chanted. Someone had brought a boom box, which was blasting classic Platinum songs at eardrum-splitting volume. The moment Kiley opened her door, two huge sheriff's deputies had stationed themselves on either side of her and escorted her through the crush. She felt like Angelina Jolie without the looks, bank account, adopted children, or hot boyfriend.

Now, staring out at the impressive sea of faces in the courtroom, waiting for the next question from the prosecutor, she wished desperately that Lydia and Esme were in the courtroom—two friendly faces to support her. But they were both stuck at work. At least Tom had shown up. He nodded encouragingly from the second row.

"Miss McCann? Are you going to answer the question?"

Startled, Kiley faced the attorney. "Excuse me?"

"I asked you if you could tell us what you saw and did on the night in question."

"Sorry. Um, so, I was out that night with my . . . my

boyfriend on the *Queen Mary*—there was a charity event—and I got a call from Sid."

The prosecutor smiled. He had to feel relieved, Kiley realized, that he was actually getting an honest answer.

"What did Sid say?"

"He told me that Serenity couldn't breathe very well, and that she was covered in what sounded to me like hives. I had him put her on the phone, and . . . and . . . she told me she had smoked some of her mother's marijuana, which she had found on a coffee table in the living room."

A collective gasp filled the courtroom.

Kiley gulped. "Anyway, that really scared me, so I called nine-one-one from the car and told them Platinum's address and what had happened to Serenity. When I arrived home, she was feeling much better but the house was swarming with police. When Platinum came home just a little while later, they arrested her."

The courtroom erupted in conversation and exclamation, and Judge Terhune banged his gavel a few times to restore order.

Kiley braved a glance at Platinum and found herself on the receiving end of a rage-filled stare. In her mind's eye, she pictured the night that Platinum had given her a beautiful white shirt right off her back so that she'd have something pretty to wear on her first real date with Tom. Then she thought about the other moments when Platinum had actually seemed to care about her.

God. What a betrayer she was. She felt terrible. What was worse—betrayal or lying? Kiley just prayed she was doing the right thing. The prosecutor asked a few more questions—had she ever seen Platinum intoxicated? Yes. Had she seen Platinum behave erratically around her children? Yes.

That was it. The prosecutor gave her over to the defense attorney for cross-examination—except there wasn't any. All Platinum's lawyer said was, "No questions," and then Kiley stepped down from the stand. Try as she might, she couldn't even look at the kids, and especially not at Platinum. Judge Terhune cleared the courtroom, then called a recess for lunch. Tom motioned to her that he'd meet her outside. She nodded gratefully. Maybe he would drive her to the beach and they could look at the porpoises from the Santa Monica Pier. That always put things in perspective.

If only life was so easy.

Spencer Lacroix, editor in chief of the *Universe,* was waiting for her outside the elevator in the lobby of the courthouse building. He held a copy of the new edition of his tabloid, and offered it to her. "For you," he said impassively. "Gratis."

Kiley took the magazine. Oh God. She was on the cover. And the picture had been taken at a very unflattering angle. Basically, it made her thighs look as though they were the size of Lake Ontario.

The headline wasn't much better.

PLATINUM NANNY HAS CLOSET FULL OF SKELETONS!

She turned to the first interior page. There were smaller inset pictures of Kiley's mom and dad—again, not looking particularly attractive—and one of Kiley picketing the model Marym Marshall's house because Marym hadn't allowed free access across her property to the beach in Malibu (how had they possibly found out about that?). And there was one final photo of her with Tom that had been taken aboard the *Queen Mary* the night of the benefit, the same night that Platinum had been arrested.

Numbly, she started reading the story as Lacroix looked on knowingly.

> Stories of Platinum's drugs-and-sex benders have been all over the place, but now it's her former nanny, Kiley McCann, whose salacious life is making headlines all its own. McCann, 17, arrived in Los Angeles in June, has already dodged one arrest and is shagging a hot model—who is romantically linked to a supermodel!
>
> Then there's the story of her alcoholic daddy back in Wisconsin, and her anxiety-ridden mother, who abandoned her teenage daughter to a life of debauchery in the City of Angels.

There was more. Lots more. Kiley felt sick all over again.

"Kiley? Let's get out of here."

She had been so engrossed in the article she hadn't heard Tom approach her. He wrapped an arm snugly around her shoulders and walked her out of the building, after noting with a look of pain the magazine that was in her hands. They emerged into the California sunlight, and he shielded her with his body from the gawkers until they reached his truck and he opened the door for her.

"It's gonna be okay," he assured her. "Stories like this come and go every day. I'll bet hardly anyone will even read it."

Kiley closed the door after her. "Thanks for the effort."

"Didn't buy it, huh?" He grinned.

"Nope."

"Had to take a shot."

"They're sure as hell going to be talking about it back in La Crosse," she replied as he started the truck. She sighed and leaned her head back. "Thank you. I think you just rescued me. Again. Can you take me out to the beach?"

"Definitely," Tom agreed.

"I've got to call my mom. She never called me back. And I was too chicken to call her again. I have to warn her so she's prepared for what people are going to say."

Kiley dug her cell out of her purse and dialed the familiar number. It rang twice, then her father picked up.

"Dad, it's me. Can I talk to Mom? It's . . . really important."

There was an uncomfortable—unbearable, really—long pause. Kiley heard her father take a sip of something before he answered her.

"Kiley." Her dad sounded disgusted. "Your mom can't speak to you right now. She's not feeling well."

For her father, that was *War and Peace*. Then, there was silence.

More silence.

"We all read it, Kiley." His voice was clipped. And angry.

"Look, I know she's mad at me, and I don't blame her, but please can you just put her on the phone? There's something I really need to tell her."

"Yeah? There's something she needs to tell you, young lady," her father seethed. "Letting you stay in California is the biggest mistake of our lives."

15

"You're sure that's the color I gave you? I'm very particular about my black."

Esme gritted her teeth, and carefully worked the tattoo needle against the small of the actress's back. In this case, the "small" of her back was named correctly. The British television star Rhetta Huff couldn't have been taller than four foot eleven, and couldn't have weighed more than ninety pounds. Yet in the past year, her dark-haired pixieish face had graced the cover of any number of magazines and television advertisements; she'd been featured on *Grey's Anatomy,* and had been asked by NBC to carry a sitcom of her own creation. They wanted so badly to be in business with her that they were willing to commit to six episodes sight unseen, reportedly at a million dollars an epi.

With all this attention and success came a great deal of money, which was why Rhetta was currently installed in one of the three presidential suites at Shutters on the Beach, the famous Santa

Monica hotel located right on the sands of the Pacific. The suite was more lavish than anything Esme had ever seen. Larger than her parents' bungalow in the Echo, it was equipped with a bedroom, living room with ocean views, powder room, bathroom with a whirlpool, dining room table for six, and overstuffed ochre and crimson furniture. Esme had taken a quick look at the rate card when Rhetta had let her in for this tattooing experience. Over three thou a night, which was more than her parents made together in two weeks.

"It's the right color," Esme assured her.

"Okay. I'm at your mercy, I suppose. I hate that."

Esme checked her watch. Just one more square quarter-inch of this tattoo to go. For eleven hundred dollars, she could put up with anything. It was ten o'clock; she'd be done by ten-thirty. She had this crazy idea to go and surprise Jonathan at his apartment, which was on the way home. It would be a reward well earned after this job. A big reward.

"For a tattoo artist, you don't talk much."

I don't talk when I don't have anything to say, Esme thought.

Then she figured she had to say something. Rhetta was paying her three hundred and fifty dollars an hour.

"Your back is beautiful."

"Aren't you a sweetheart." Like every other star Esme had ever met, Rhetta got nicer the moment she heard a compliment. "Would you like to take a break? They have a smashing room-service menu."

"No, I'm on a roll here." Esme's tools were spread out around her; the electrical cord running from the wall to her needle snaked over the dining room. She could say this for tiny Rhetta: the British girl had guts. There hadn't been a single peep of pain since Esme had started the procedure three hours before, and there hadn't been a drop of alcohol on Rhetta's breath, either. "You've got a high tolerance for pain."

"I think I'm light on that gene. I don't even like novocaine at the dentist. Has certain advantages, really. Broke my ankle on a set once and didn't realize it until the dresser pointed out that my left shoe didn't want to come off. They were Manolos, too. Close to done?"

"Yep. Just hold still." Esme finished the last character, dabbing with a sterile pad at the blood she raised. "You know the drill for care of one of these?"

Rhetta nodded. "You saw the one on my ankle? A month for it to heal. Wash four to five times a day with antibacterial soap. Pat it dry. Antibacterial cream to follow."

"Bacitracin. And stay out of the sun. You'll be ready to rumble by the end of September."

"Brilliant. You'll find cash in an envelope on the table. Do you have any business cards? I'm sure I can make some referrals."

Esme smiled. She'd finally had some cards printed at Landmark Print and Copy in Sherman Oaks, which Jonathan had said was the best print shop in the city. She and the owner had designed a simple dove gray card with just Esme's name in raised print, her cell number, and the words "Body Art" printed continuously around the four edges of the card. She extracted one from her jeans pocket and handed it to Rhetta.

"Give me ten," the actress insisted. "And get ready for your phone to start ringing. Just don't abandon me when you're rich and famous."

When she was rich and famous? That was a joke, coming from a hot actress like Rhetta. But still. It made Esme feel good. She decided that this evening had been something of a test. It was one thing to do tattoos for the boys in the Echo, or even for Jonathan and his actor friends. Or even for someone like Jacqueline, who approached her at the club. It was another to do one when a friend of a quasi-friend called, as Rhetta had, out of the blue. And when, at first blush anyway, she didn't care for the friend of the quasi-friend at all.

She'd gotten the envelope with the money and was just about to leave when Rhetta stopped her with her posh British voice. "Esme? Can I give you some unsolicited advice?"

She wanted to say no but didn't. "Sure."

"You're a great artist. And you seem like a nice person. But coming to people's hotel rooms to do tattoos? By yourself? A bit dodgy, luv. You're getting paid well. Bring a big strong guy and pay him twenty bucks an hour just to sit there and look hot. It's a bargain, for what you're getting paid. And you'll be in a better position when the person who answers the door turns out to be Rhett instead of Rhetta. If you catch my drift." Rhetta put her palms up, in a gesture that said to Esme that she might have been talking from personal experience.

Esme nodded. It really *was* a good idea. Then she thanked Rhetta again, wished her luck with her career, and headed out into the hotel hallway. Ten minutes later, she had the Goldhagens' new Aston Martin tooling up Ocean Avenue toward Jonathan's apartment. Miraculously, there was a spot on the street across from his building, and she did a U-turn on Ocean Avenue and pulled in. She'd only been to his apartment—an underdecorated one-bedroom in this exclusive location—a few times. Most of those times, they had ended up making intense love atop his billiards table.

From where she was parked, she could see up to his eighth-floor oceanfront apartment. All the lights were blazing, which she took as a very good sign he'd be home. Maybe she could surprise him.

But when she buzzed his buzzer, there was no answer. Strange. He had to be in the shower, or something. She buzzed a couple more times; he still didn't answer. So when a young white couple in their twenties obviously dressed for clubbing came out the front door, Esme flashed them a winning grin, walked as if she belonged there despite her low-key, ideal-for-tattooing jeans-and-blue-work shirt combination, and slipped in through the open door.

So much for security. It made Esme think once again that Rhetta was right; maybe she should start doing jobs with a guy escort. Or maybe she should just forget about what her mother said and open her own studio—not one of those sleazoid ones like you'd find in the Echo or in the far reaches of the Valley, or—gasp!—on Hollywood near Vine. No, an upscale one, maybe in a discreet office in Century City, or near CAA or Endeavor. That'd be cool. Stars would come to see their agents, and stop off for some body art on the way to Yoga Booty.

Jonathan's lobby belied the opulence of the apartments. Stark white, with just some framed photographs of Santa Monica in the fifties on the walls. There was a Latino doorman reading the *Hollywood Reporter*, but he merely waved to Esme as she headed for the elevators. Esme figured he must have thought she was hired help for someone. The wood-paneled elevator was open, and she took it to the eighth floor. Jonathan's apartment was to the right at the end of the hall. As Esme approached it, she heard music: Astrud Gilberto, the Brazilian singer. She grinned. She'd been the one to introduce her music to Jonathan. And now, he was playing it? Nice.

She rang his buzzer. No answer. She rang again. Still no answer. But there was definitely music.

"Jonath—"

She started to call his name when the door swung open. There was Jonathan, wearing nothing but a white terry cloth robe. And there was Tarshea behind him, wearing nothing but a white terry cloth towel.

Anger didn't begin to describe the tsunami of white-hot rage that crashed over Esme. He was cheating on her. No—Tarshea had stolen him. She had stolen her job, and now she was stealing her boyfriend. Jonathan opened his mouth to speak but Esme beat him to it.

"Don't even try to explain," she snapped. "There's nothing to explain."

She swallowed the rage, mostly because she didn't want to look at his puke-worthy face for one more instant. As for the life-stealer Tarshea, she could go back to Jamaica and rot, for all Esme cared.

She got into the Goldhagens' car, but she didn't drive home. Instead, she went to an Internet café she knew of on the Third Street Promenade. The promenade was full of lovers and strollers at this hour, gathered around the street musicians and performers out passing the hat. The café was full, so Esme had to wait for a computer.

It didn't matter how long it was. It could have been an hour, it could have been a day. The rage turned to numbness and back to rage again. So many people had warned her. Her mother had warned her. Jorge had warned her. Even her old boyfriend, Junior, had warned her, in his own way.

But no. She thought she knew better. She knew she knew better. And where did it get her? To this Internet café she'd never been in before, as angry as she'd ever been. She tried to direct the anger at Jonathan. And still, a lot of it came right back to herself. She was such an idiot.

She didn't notice the iced tea for a long time. When she did see it, she drank it quickly. And then, she started to type. It was an e-mail she realized she'd been composing from the moment Jonathan opened his door.

To: StevenGoldhagen@goldhagenproductions.com
From: ESMEC@hotmail.com
Subject: Resignation

Steve and Diane,

I've thought about it a lot, and I am going to resign as nanny to Easton and Weston effective as soon as possible, but no longer than two weeks from today. There are several reasons that I am doing this, and because you have been kind to me and to my parents I think it is important to explain my reasoning. I want you to know first that I have given this a great deal of thought and that it is not a decision I am making rashly. Most importantly, you have a very good nanny already. Tarshea is wonderful with the children and very responsible.

Second, I thought that I would want to attend Bel Air High School. But I have to say that I am not comfortable there and that my first experiences with the school have not been good ones. I think that I will be more comfortable at my same school in Echo Park instead of doing my senior year with kids I don't know at all.

Third—

Esme stopped writing. Was it the Goldhagens' business that her tattoo venture was taking off, and that she wasn't even sure she was interested in going to college? No. It wasn't any of their business. So she didn't do the third paragraph, just wrote some general stuff that she hoped wouldn't get them too upset with her or with her parents. But even if they did get upset with her parents, or even fired them, Esme knew that with her income from tattooing she could support her entire family. They could probably move out of the Echo to someplace like South Pasadena or Eagle Rock, if they wanted.

So she finished the e-mail, signed it, and sent it. Even as she did, she realized that she never addressed the real reason for her quitting: Jonathan. She resolved that if the Goldhagens asked her any questions at all, she would just refer them to their son.

16

Monday night, Lydia thought, would be a perfect night for a fantasy date. And she planned it as carefully as the Amas planned a jaguar hunt.

First, she arranged for X to pick Billy up at his home in Mar Vista, and to have a thermos of martinis in the car in case Billy's lips were parched—X was driving, so he was on a strict Vitamin Water diet. There'd be no frustration dealing with the traffic, and Billy could just relax. Second, X would drop him off here, at Royce Hall on the UCLA campus, where Billy would no doubt do an extended double take at the marquee's double booking: Chick Corea and Béla Fleck. These were two of Billy's favorite jazz musicians in a one-night-only, very special performance. Billy might even think this was some sort of a hoax.

But it would get even better. There would be a theater employee outside the box office who would hold up a discreet sign that read BILLY MARTIN and would request appropriate ID. And when Billy handed over his driver's license, he would be shocked by the front-row ticket presented to him . . . a ticket for a seat right next to the resplendent, gracious, and exceedingly hot, ever-humble Lydia Chandler.

After the concert, well, there were a myriad of possibilities. The best ended up in her guesthouse at Kat's estate. Without Anya in the picture, who could possibly object?

Now, all the lucky SOB had to do was show up. Where the hell was he?

The ushers cycled the lobby lights so that everyone would take their seats; the concert was about to begin. Lydia had come dressed in a lavender knee-length Ella Moss Havana dress that she borrowed from Anya's half-emptied closet. And she didn't care if the queen of the gulag would be pissed that it was gone.

Billy still hadn't shown up when the house lights dimmed and the audience applauded Fleck and Corea's entrance. She had to figure out what was going on. She shimmied past the other patrons in her row, and then up the aisle. Where was he? Maybe the ticket dude had abandoned his post. She was ready to kill him.

But no. The guy was still at his post. Huh. Lydia started to worry. Maybe they'd been in a horrible traffic accident. She took out her cell to call X, then cursed loudly and repeatedly. The battery was dead.

What to do, what to do? She couldn't even call X; she had no idea what his number was, she always just speed-dialed. Same thing with Billy. Maybe Billy's number was listed. She stepped out of the theater into the warm, jasmine-scented night air, with the thought that maybe she could find a pay phone.

Pay dirt. There was one about a hundred feet away. She started across the asphalt toward it, then stopped.

A familiar pair of silhouetted shoulders was slumped on a bench just ahead, directly beneath an old-fashioned gaslit lamppost.

"Billy! Why aren't you inside?"

No response, not even a look. Bad sign. Why?

Lydia was careful to keep her voice even. "The concert just started. Are you okay?"

"Why did you do it?"

"Do what? These tickets?" Lydia plopped down on the bench with him. He didn't move to take her hand or put an arm around her. Bad sign number two.

"You know what I mean. Why did you *lie*? About Luis, about sleeping with him, about everything?"

She instinctively tried to cover. "Did that crazy boy try to contact you? We already went over this. There was never anything between us. He's just jealous. Whatever you heard from him was just the sound of his ego—or something—deflating, and—"

"*Don't* lie again. Not this time. Please? Isn't it enough that I know the truth? I just want to hear it from you." Now, for the first time, he turned to look at her. His eyes weren't really that angry. What were they? Ah. They were sad. Lydia had seen the facial expression before, in the jungle, when her father was forced to treat an Ama man suffering from a particularly dangerous snakebite. Her father knew, and the man knew, that the bite would ultimately be fatal.

Just like this encounter could be.

"It's a simple question. What happened between you and Luis?"

Lydia could feel her eyes welling up. She wouldn't cry. "I don't know what you're talking about."

Billy sighed. "Fine. Since you won't answer, I'll answer for you. You lied about being a virgin, you lied about sleeping with Luis, and you're lying right now." He stood. "I don't care about the bullshit you lied about. But I do care that you lied. Being honest isn't that hard. But you know who I had to hear this from? Jimmy."

Jimmy? How would he—

He must have overheard her talking on the phone to Luis that night when he'd called Kat's house. No wonder he'd been acting so strange.

"Yeah, Jimmy. Think about that, Lydia. And if that makes you feel like shit . . . good."

Billy turned, jammed his hands in his pockets, and left.

There were a million things she could have said—that she was just trying to protect what they had, that she was embarrassed by her mistake. But she couldn't even bring herself to call after him. The problem was, he was right. And she *did* feel like shit. All she could do was watch his silhouette disappear into the night.

An hour later, despondent Lydia was on the same bench when the attendant from the theater came running out to her.

"Miss?"

"Yes?"

"There is a young man waiting for you in the parking lot. He has a black Beemer. He says his name is X. He called the box office and asked me to look for you."

"Thank you." Lydia pressed some crumpled bills into his hand. "Thank you very much."

152

The ride home with X was silent; he offered no words of encouragement, Lydia offered no words of explanation. All she wanted was to get back to her guesthouse without running into anyone, especially her mother. If she kept herself in this trance she could make it to bed. Tomorrow would be another day. She'd work something out. She always did.

He dropped her in front of the main house, and she decided not to go through it. Instead, she cut around the back, past the pool and the hot tub, past the tennis court, where there'd be less chance that she'd encounter anyone with a pulse.

No such luck. There was someone in the hot tub. Her mother.

"Hey, sweet pea! The water's amazing—come on in!"

Shit. But she couldn't very well say no. So after some perfunctory greetings that she hoped her mother would mistake for plain tiredness, she stripped and climbed in. Being naked in the water with her mother was nothing new. They used to swim together in the Rio Negro all the time. At first, they'd worn bathing suits, but the Amas looked at them as though they were nuts. A week or two later, they'd gone native.

It was a strange comfort to be once again skinny-dipping with her mom, even though it was now in the lap of luxury instead of the warm waters of Amazonia. She sank into one corner of the enormous redwood tub, which was embedded in the Pernambuco deck. It gave her a little comfort to know that the wood, at least, had been harvested in Brazil.

They soaked in silence for a time. More than once, Lydia was about to confess that she'd been dumped, that it was all her fault, and that it hurt to breathe. But what came out was "Um, pretty nice night, huh?"

Lydia remembered her first day at Aunt Kat's mansion: lounging in the sun by the swimming pool without a care in the world; the fundamentals of human survival in the jungle banished from her mind. The novelty of it all had worn off faster than Lydia could have predicted.

"Yes. It's beautiful."

"It's amazing how fast you get used to it." Lydia arched her neck against the redwood and stared into the heavens.

"Honestly, I doubt I'll have the time. I'm flying back to Manaus as soon as Kat comes back from the U.S. Open. That's right after Labor Day."

Lydia felt a pang of sorrow. Billy had kicked her to the curb. She needed her mom more than ever.

She couldn't help it. A tear rolled down her face.

"Don't worry, sweetie," her mother assured her. "You can always write, and I'll call you whenever I'm in Manaus. And we've got FedEx now. So tell your mom what's going on."

Lydia did. Right from the start. With her and Billy. Her and Luis. Her and Billy. "Billy dumped me tonight, and he was right because it was my fault."

"You can always, always come back if you want."

"To the Amazon? God no!" Lydia blanched.

Her mother laughed. "Good. We both know why you're here. Don't give it up without a fight."

There was an ice-filled caddy attached to the hot tub; inside were bottles of water, juice, and beer. Lydia opened an Anchor Steam; her mother just smiled.

"Want one?" Lydia asked. "I don't think the Amas are making these."

154

Karen shook her head. "I haven't had a beer since we moved to the jungle. No reason to start now."

Lydia took a contemplative swallow. "You didn't have to go there, you know."

"Maybe not. You know, Lydia, I don't think I've ever told you this. Even though it was your dad who came up with the idea to move us to the Amazon, I'm the one who made the final decision. I *wanted* to go."

"What?"

This was shocking news. Lydia put her beer can down on the edge of the tub. Maybe she should switch to something stronger. Not vodka—maybe something radioactive.

"I always thought you hated it there as much as I did."

"Well, I didn't want you to hold it against me. If it helps, I did hate it. At least at first. I missed my friends in Texas. I made your father angry when I didn't know what I was doing with a patient. I'd get the Amas angry when I wouldn't eat anaconda or monkey meat. Like that."

"Been there, done that," Lydia commiserated. "I remember when the Ama kids used to make fun of me because I wanted to wear shoes."

"Right, sorry. The point is, all those failures are now fond memories. Does that make any sense?"

"Not really. I still feel like shit. And Billy still hates my guts." Lydia drained her beer. Then she cracked open another as her mother climbed out of the pool and wrapped a soft black towel around herself.

"You could try apologizing to him," her mom said as she dried her hair with another towel.

"I think it's too late," Lydia said sadly.

Her mom put a finger under Lydia's chin and tipped her daughter's head so that she could look into her eyes. "Okay, so you made a mistake, sweet pea. You live and you learn. I'm proud because of who you are. Growing up in the rain forest—that's made you unique. You're one of the strongest people I know."

Lydia felt an unfamiliar ache at the back of her heart. "Thanks, Mom. I mean it."

She closed her eyes and sank into the hot water. She didn't feel strong right now, but she knew she could be strong. As strong as her mother thought. Maybe stronger.

She'd screwed up. But she was alive. In the rain forest, she'd learned that as long as you were alive, you still had a chance. Fine. A chance was all she wanted. A chance was all she needed.

17

When she woke up on Tuesday morning, Kiley was almost as nervous about Platinum's testimony planned for that day as she had been about her own. She envisioned some sort of Courtney Love–style meltdown—a string of expletives so rude, crude, and socially unacceptable that Judge Terhune might put her in jail for the longest contempt-of-court sentence in the history of Western jurisprudence.

"All rise, the honorable Judge Terhune presiding."

The bailiff's voice snapped Kiley into the moment. She was in the courtroom gallery again, with Serenity on her left and Sid on her right. Since her testimony the day before, the kids had barely spoken to her. They were that furious over her "betrayal." She had tried in vain to explain why she had told the truth; their reply was that she must hate their mother, and how much was the colonel paying her under the table?

Judge Terhune strode in and sat. Everyone else sat too, with the usual murmurs of anticipation. The star witness was about to be called to testify. This was going to be great. But the judge surveyed the courtroom before he allowed any witnesses to be called.

"Ladies and gentlemen, this morning I met with representatives from the Los Angeles Police Department," he intoned. "Apparently, there has been some sort of problem in the evidence room at the police station downtown. Last night, all of the evidence in this case went missing. All of it. Whether it was lost, misplaced, pilfered, or sold on eBay, our friends at the LAPD can't explain it."

The reaction from the courtroom drowned out Judge Terhune's gavel. Cell phones came out and people started shouting, despite the judge's repeated pleas for quiet. Kiley saw Platinum conferring intently with her lawyer, while Sid and Serenity high-fived each other so hard that they momentarily forgot their animus toward Kiley.

"What's this mean?" Serenity said over and over. "What does this mean?"

"I don't know!" Kiley's answer was honest.

Finally, Terhune was able to restore order, though he practically had to wear out his gavel to do it. "I want to strongly state that in my mind there is no question about the guilt or innocence of the defendant. Were I a member of the jury, I would vote for her guilt."

Kiley took in the members of the jury. They were nodding in unison like twelve bobbleheads.

"That said, with the actual physical evidence no longer in the possession of the police, I am bound by precedent and statute to dismiss this case with prejudice, even if it is against my better judgment." He rapped his gavel one more time. "Case dismissed!"

It was over. The courtroom erupted into bedlam. Platinum charged toward her younger children and scooped one into each arm for a bear hug. The colonel stormed the prosecutor's table and berated him at the top of his lungs for botching an open-and-shut case. Kiley stayed in her seat and just took it all in.

She felt a rush of . . . what? Relief? Confusion? Sure, the case was over. But she couldn't help but dread her own present and future. After all, she had told the truth when she testified. The kids hated her. No doubt Platinum did, too.

Then, something unexpected happened. Something so unbelievable, in fact, that Kiley briefly considered the possibility that she was having a hallucination brought on by stress—a strange form of panic attack that she'd never experienced before. Platinum had one hand on Sid's shoulder and one on her daughter as she talked with her lawyer. Then, she spun toward Kiley and beckoned for her to join them. Kiley did, with some trepidation. She expected Platinum to rip her a new orifice.

Quite the opposite. "Kids, you guys owe Kiley a goddamn apology," Platinum demanded.

"What?" Serenity was aghast.

"She's the one who should be apologizing to us. And to you! She's the one who trashed you to the court," Sid protested. "We didn't do anything wrong."

"Oh, come on. You two are full of shit," Platinum responded coolly, if profanely. The court officers looked aghast. But there was nothing they could do.

Sid was livid. "This is bullshit. She was gonna put you in jail, Mom! She got up there and told them all those stories that made you look like a bad parent. She's a bitch. You should fire her."

"Have you kids been brainwashed by my brother-in-law? She's the only thing that's kept you guys sane since I was away. Come on! What the hell is wrong with you?"

All that Kiley wished was that she could whip out her cell phone and record this for Esme and Lydia.

The rock star nudged Sid in the back. "Do it."

Sid cleared his throat. "I'm sorry, Kiley. I guess we haven't been very nice to you lately."

"Serenity?" Platinum prompted.

"Me too. I—"

Platinum cut off her own daughter. "That's enough. No need to go fucking overboard."

"I accept," Kiley said, with mock solemnity, since she caught a glimpse of the colonel and Susan. They were standing side by side in the gallery, observing the proceedings in stony silence.

"All right, now let's get the hell outta here. I can't wait to get home." Platinum put an arm around Kiley. "I've had the Lotus parked in a garage around the corner, waiting for my acquittal. This is just as good. Come on, Kiley. You're riding with me."

Platinum pulled her red Lotus through the security gate, then up the driveway to her estate. She screeched to a halt in front of the garage, where a film crew from MTV awaited her.

"What the . . . ?" Kiley was aghast. How had they possibly gotten to the house so quickly? Who had let them in?

Platinum grinned. "No worries, I called them. A little bird

told my lawyer what was going to go down in court this morning, so I thought I'd make a couple of calls and prepare myself a proper homecoming."

"But . . . but . . . you looked so shocked when the judge made his announcement."

"Honey, haven't you heard? I'm not just a singer, I'm an actress." Platinum unfolded her endless legs from the Lotus and waved to the cameras. "Goddamn holy shit, it feels good to be home!"

"So tell us, Platinum. Were you afraid you might end up in jail?" Kiley recognized the reporter from MTV News.

"Are you kidding? I'm as innocent as a virgin in a nunnery on a remote Pacific island. I knew justice would be served, I just had to wait it out, you know?"

She gestured for the crew to follow her into the house's grand foyer, which featured floor-to-ceiling mirrors on opposite walls, white-on-white decor, and a plush white faux-fur rug. The kids, the colonel, and Susan hadn't yet arrived. Or else the colonel had made a snap decision to take them all away to San Diego.

"So how do you feel now, seeing your home again?"

"I'm just glad to be with my kids," Platinum demurred. "And, you know, to have my pool, and my wardrobe, and food prepared by my a-ma-zing chef, Mrs. Cleveland! Mrs. Cleveland, take a bow!"

The cook, who had poked her head around a corner to glance at the new arrivals, took an awkward bow and then scuttled back to the kitchen. Platinum turned back to the reporter. "Of course, you simply *must* join us for dinner. There's nothing like a good old-fashioned family meal at my house! But let me give you the tour first."

A half hour later, after a *Cribs*-style tour of the white-on-white master bedroom, the kids' rooms, the home studio, the gym, and the lavish gardens filled with gardenias, jasmine, and other fragrant white flowers, Platinum made good on her offer. She ushered the charmed MTV crew into the dining room—same white-on-white design—where an enormous buffet table groaned under the weight of a welcome-home feast worthy of, well, an international celebrity. Bruce, Serenity, and Sid were there now too, and Platinum made the appropriate introductions.

"I made all your favorites," Mrs. Cleveland announced proudly. "Grilled baby squid in black-bean sauce, nori rolls, kalamata angel hair with baby artichokes, sweet potato fries, beef tenderloin stuffed with blue crab, pancetta-wrapped asparagus with lemon hollandaise, tuna tartar with Ethiopian herbs, Thai coconut-milk soup with tiger shrimp, an all-white root vegetable gratin, and for dessert, baked Alaska with coffee ice cream and Ghirardelli fudge. Oh, and Wolfgang dropped by with some lobster rolls and a dulce de leche cheesecake. He sends his love."

"Holy crap, Mrs. Cleveland, you have outdone yourself. But no way we can eat all this. Call the women's shelter downtown and see if we can send over our leftovers." Platinum collapsed dramatically into a white leather armchair at the head of the table and popped a piece of sushi into her mouth.

"I already did call, but they're getting food from some CAA party tonight. I'll see what else I can do."

"So Platinum, what's next on your professional agenda?" the reporter asked through a mouthful of garlic smashed potatoes with white truffle butter. Kiley noted that her boss had poured herself a champagne flute of sparkling juice, not champagne. Was this a sign of change?

"Well, obviously, my first priority is to reacquaint myself with my beautiful children." Platinum was deliberately low-key. She beamed at her kids, and they beamed right back. "But after that, I'm not going back into the studio for a while."

"You're not?" The MTV reporter was surprised.

"Hell no. I'm branching out. Into literature."

"The next Rimbaud?"

"The next Dr. Goddamn Seuss. I'm writing a children's book. All about a goose being falsely accused of a crime, and the vindication of justice. A platinum goose. I started it in detention."

Okay. This was genius.

"But that won't happen until I've had a to-die-for guava-pineapple facial at LeSpa."

"I don't want to hear about her and her damn facials!" Kiley heard the colonel's familiar voice thunder in the hallway outside the kitchen.

Platinum grinned. "Well, well, well, if it isn't Private Ryan himself. May I ask what the hell you're doing in my house?"

Oh yeah. Her boss was back. Sharp-eyed, loud-voiced, and a hundred percent tact-free. But the colonel didn't budge an inch. Meanwhile, the reporter and the camera dude grinned at each other. This was obviously the kind of footage they'd been hoping for.

"I'm here to try and talk some sense into you. You may have fooled the court, but you and I both know you don't know the first thing about responsible parenting. Therefore, I am here to suggest that you let me keep doing what I've been doing during your absence. Providing a strict, moral environment for your children."

Whoa. Kiley watched the storm break over her boss's lovely face. Nobody told Platinum what to do, especially in her own home. Especially not a poker-up-the-yahooligan like her brother-in-law. Kiley braced for the inevitable explosion. But it never came. Instead, Platinum stood up, smoothed her cascading hair into place, and took a couple of steps toward her sister and the colonel.

"Susan, you're my sister. Feel free to hang out as long as you want. Colonel, I no longer require your assistance. So I will kindly ask you to go." She looked at her watch. "By 1300 hours. That's in five minutes." Platinum grinned her familiar mischievous grin. "And turn in your keys and your weapon on the way out and don't let the door hit you in the ass. You're getting a dishonorable discharge."

18

"Just talk to them, okay?" Karen pleaded.

Lydia thumbed through a few pages in the *Harper's Bazaar* she'd gleaned from the mail pile on the counter and didn't respond.

Like any demanding chore, it had to be done sooner or later. It would mean sitting Jimmy and Martina down, buttering them up with all the high-octane, sugary snacks they could stomach—there were some advantages to not having Anya around—and confessing to them both why she was the world's biggest fool-lowlife-lying-sumbitch. Or words to that effect.

Well, confessing to Martina. Jimmy already knew why. For him, it would be a confirmation.

"All right. How about after Billy takes Jimmy to the skate park down in Venice?" Lydia sipped from her nonalcoholic piña colada smoothie. At least the new morning cook made superb breakfast beverages.

Before she could respond any further, the kids stampeded into the kitchen.

"Hi guys! You want something to eat? I can get Juanita to fix up some poached eggs, or bowls of cereal with real milk . . . ," Lydia said as the kids pulled two stools to the island counter. What did the kids know? And when did they know about it? How much info had Jimmy shared with Martina?

Quite a bit. Martina looked right at her with sad eyes. "Is the reason that Billy's so mad at you because you cheated on him with the golf pro?"

Ouch. Best to treat it like a flesh wound with an old bandage on it. One fierce tug, bleeding be damned.

She looked right at her cousin. "Yes, Martina. And then I lied to him about it. And he found out and he dumped me. I'm a jerk and I feel like swamp scum. Let it be a lesson for you."

The kids just stared at her with cold eyes.

"Will you at least acknowledge that you heard me? It's hard to have a conversation if I'm the only one talking."

Lydia snapped her fingers in the air. Nothing. Okay.

"But didn't you tell us that you should be honest with somebody if you really like them?" Martina asked, her voice small.

"I did, but—"

"You know what that makes you?" Jimmy scowled. "You know what it's called when you tell somebody one thing and do the opposite? It's called a hypocrite."

Lydia sighed. At least the kid's vocabulary was on track. "Why don't we all go out for ice cream this afternoon, and we can talk about it some more? That'll be fun, right?"

Martina's eyebrows lifted into a look that could have passed for hopeful, but the reaction from Jimmy was quite different. He merely slid off his stool and stepped out of the kitchen. A moment later, his sister followed him. Great. Both kids were official card-carrying members of the I-hate-Lydia-Chandler fan club. And why not? After all, it was the second major breakup they'd been forced to watch without any say in the last two weeks. And while they knew better than to use their mom—who was off in New York for the U.S. Open—as a punching bag, their nanny cousin wasn't nearly so off-limits.

"Excuse me, Mom," she told her mother. "I'm out of here."

"I don't blame you. Don't worry. It'll pass."

"I'm not so sure."

Lydia got up from the table and moved into the hallway, gliding a finger along some of the mansion's featured mementos: the photo of Kat and Anya shaking hands at the French Open back when they were competitors; the teak totemic carving that had been a gift from Karen for their fifth anniversary; the weird gargoyle Anya had brought back from a trip to Russia. The moms did have a certain sense of style, but Lydia couldn't imagine accumulating so much stuff with anybody.

The doorbell rang. Lydia heard Jimmy run to answer it. She knew who it was and drifted toward the door like a condemned person who knew there was no choice but to stagger to the gallows. Billy was dressed for a morning with Jimmy at the skate park, in a Sonic Youth T-shirt and torn jeans.

"Hi," she tried.

"Yo."

It didn't take a doctorate in behavioral psychology to understand that Billy also wanted to get out of there as soon as possible. He rearranged invisible pebbles on the floor with his Vans sneakers. He clamped his hands beneath his elbows. His eyes wandered from five different knickknacks in five seconds: the antique umbrella stand, the walnut coffee table, the pair of porcelain pigeons, the Tiffany lampshade, the painting by Gustav Klimt. Anywhere to keep from looking at Lydia.

Fair enough. She couldn't do a thing if he wanted to react by smoldering. But seeing him so agitated wasn't easy, especially since it was essentially her fault.

Thankfully, Jimmy soon reappeared with his skateboard. Even before Lydia could unglue her tongue from the bottom of her mouth to wish them a nice time at the park, the guys were on their way. The only acknowledgment of Lydia's presence was the extra force with which Jimmy shut the door on his way out.

"It'll be okay." Lydia heard her mother's voice behind her. "Kind of reminds me of accidentally violating an Amarakaire taboo. Even *they* eventually got over a grudge. Those boys will too."

If her mom thought that her words would be comforting, she was wrong. But Lydia acknowledged the attempt. "Thanks, Mom. But if they had a million other people they could turn to, the Amas would've kept on grudging. I might get Jimmy back. He kind of needs me. Billy? He's gone for good."

"I wish I could help, sweetie," Karen said. "But I know something that might make you feel better." She handed Lydia a bulging envelope addressed to her; the return address was Bel Air High School. "This came in the mail yesterday."

"Don't tell me. They're trying to send me more goofy shirts." Lydia ran a finger under the flap and looked at the mailing from her new high school. Inside were more papers, packets, pamphlets, and registration materials than she cared to see. It was like a treasure trove of Ama toilet paper.

"Do they really expect me to read all this?" Lydia asked.

Karen smiled widely. "No, honey. They expect you to fill it out."

Back in the Amazon, Lydia had been schooled with her own set of standards, and was answerable only to her mother and father. English literature applied equally to the rare novels that made their way upriver and the air-dropped magazines she craved. Study about botany meant talking about biochemistry, since the shaman's herbs were at least as potent as conventional medications. The simple mathematics of Ama bartering doubled as anthropology and tripled as home economics. And pretty much all "core subjects" included what Bel Air High School would have parsed out as physical education.

"What's the big deal? I go to their school, they teach me what they want, and the rest is just details. Can't you fill this out for me?"

Karen laughed. "It's not as simple as that. You're going to have to start thinking about SATs, ACTs, and college applications."

"How about the track team?"

Her mother looked at her blankly.

"Bad joke." Lydia rubbed a point of tension that was developing between her eyebrows. She thought again how simple life was in the rain forest. You were born. You lived. You hunted. You died.

"Tell you what. Jimmy will be with Billy until the afternoon. Martina's about to go to the club with Faith. I was listening to the radio," her mother said, "and KLOS says it's going to be beautiful. I could use a change of venue. Whaddaya say?"

Lydia smiled wanly. "Why not?"

• • •

Since Lydia didn't have a driver's license, and Karen's had expired years ago, X shuttled them to an outdoor restaurant at the corner of Sunset Plaza and Sunset Boulevard, a place called Café Med. It offered fine Italian cuisine as easy on the eyes as on the palate. The imported-from-Rome waitstaff and the imported-from-across-the-pond Eurotrash clientele were easy on the eyes, too. Not that Lydia was back in the market after Billy's have-a-nice-life. But it never hurt to look.

They sat under the awning of the shaded patio. Almost immediately, Lydia spotted a trio of soap opera stars from *The Bold and the Beautiful,* and two members of the Decemberists, but knew that stargazing was a concept lost to her mother outside of the night sky.

Karen marveled at the menu. "I remember this. Having options. We've eaten a lot of monkey and turtle meat lately. The peacock bass haven't been biting this summer. The river is too high."

"You sound like me when I first got here," Lydia said. After Karen gleefully decided on an arugula salad and a one-person pizza with four cheeses, and Lydia chose a sliced portobello mushroom sandwich on homemade Italian bread, she started to go through the materials from the high school packet that she had brought along.

It was daunting. There had to be two dozen memos, all of which dealt with a different aspect of the minutiae of high school. Earthquake emergency. Homeland Security emergency. Parking permits. (*Like that would ever matter,* she thought). Discipline code. Drug policy. The list went on and on. And on. Then Lydia scanned the list of required materials for all new students: school supplies, gym clothes, approved locks for her hallway locker and gym locker, insurance information, previous school transcripts (well, that wasn't happening), a photo for her ID card, and choice of meal plan and degree plan. Then there was the course work: Would she like the advanced placement English course, or the single-semester English IV course? U.S. history or world history? Physics or chemistry?

The boxed aphorism on the front page of the course catalog put it all in perspective. "Choose wisely. After all, we're talking about the rest of your life here."

Great.

"If they need some information about your homeschooling, I can come in to talk to them," her mother offered.

"That'd be good, I guess." Lydia's voice was somber as a buff Italian waiter in black jeans and black silk shirt brought them their food.

"You okay, hon? You seem down." Her mother tasted the pizza. "Wow! How's yours?"

Lydia stared at the portobello mushroom sandwich dripping with fresh lemon juice and garnished with peach slices. It should have been delicious. But her appetite was gone.

"Talk to me, Lydia," her mother urged.

She did. The words tumbled out of her faster than she intended them to, thoughts running into each other, muttering the way some of the Amas did when they chewed too many coca leaves. "It feels like pretty much everything is going to shit. I mean, last night my friend Esme was talking about how she quit working at the Goldhagens' and won't even be going to high school. So she won't be there with me. The only girls I met hate Kiley. They could decide to hate me, too. What I did to Billy proves that I'm an idiot, which is exactly the way the kids think of me. Why would I think that when Kat comes back she'll even want me to be their nanny? I don't do pity parties, Mom. I don't. But right now, I wouldn't mind an invitation."

She pinched her fingertips, swallowed hard, and forced a smile before glancing around the restaurant to see if anyone had witnessed her miniature breakdown. Fortunately not. The soap opera trio was deep in conversation, and the musicians were huddled over some contracts spread out on their table. Good. At least her humiliation wasn't public.

Her mother rubbed her chin, then scooted her wrought-iron chair closer to Lydia. "I'm honored."

"Huh?"

"You're not a girl anymore, Lydia. I'm honored that you'd share your feelings with me. It's not like your father and I gave you a normal upbringing."

Lydia looked across Sunset Boulevard, and then south into Los Angeles. The day was clear; the city spread out like some sort of enormous mother ship. She wondered, *Who's to say that this is normal and the Amazon is bizarre?* Los Angeles had its own tribes and strange mating rituals. In some ways, Amazonia made more sense.

It was a thought funny enough to make her laugh.

"What's so funny?" Karen asked.

"What would the head shaman think of this place?" Lydia said.

"He'd probably want to order everything on the menu," Karen declared.

Lydia laughed again. "What am I going to do when you go back to the Amazon?"

Karen raised her brows, frowning. "I've been wondering

172

about that myself, sweetie. And to be honest, I kind of like it here. I don't know if I want to leave so soon." She picked up Lydia's sandwich as if it was made of gold. "Sure, it's a little smoggy. But you can eat bread here without baking it yourself."

"That's true," Lydia allowed. "But it also has little cousins that think you're the enemy."

"Martina and Jimmy, you mean."

"Exactly."

Her mother had ordered an iced tea—she half drained it before she answered. "Can I give you some motherly advice?"

"You can give me *any* advice."

"If you take a bite of that sandwich."

"Fine." Lydia took a huge bite. Fantastic. Then another. And another. By the third bite, she decided she was ravenous.

"I forgot my camera," her mother lamented. "I'd like to take a picture to show your dad."

Lydia handed over her cell. "It's nothing fancy, just a Samsung. But you can take pictures with it . . . after I hear your advice."

Her mother sighed. "You'll have to teach me how to take a cell phone picture. As for the advice, it's pretty simple. Jimmy is going to stay mad at you for a long time. He feels betrayed, and he thinks Billy is his bud. Your best ally, though, is Martina. She's pretty wise for a girl her age."

"She's a baby!"

"That doesn't mean she's not wise. She grew up with Anya as one of her mothers. She's used to adversity. Here's my advice."

Lydia leaned forward to listen to her mother's simple words: "See if she can help you."

19

Jonathan and Tarshea.

His hands pulling off her clothes, the length of her underneath him as he stared down into her eyes and—

She felt like throwing up. She'd felt that way ever since she'd walked in on the boy she loved—had *thought* she loved—who was cheating on her with—dammit to hell!—the girl she'd championed and helped bring to America.

How, how, how could she have been so wrong, so stupid, so utterly *ingenuous*? All the feelings she'd had five years ago, when she'd found that her very first boyfriend had only *pretended* to love her so that he could use her in a drive-by gangbanger murder, came rushing back to her.

She had trusted Jonathan. Loved him. Lied to the Goldhagens and defied her parents to be with him.

Nothing—*nothing* could feel as bad as knowing he didn't care.

Esme hadn't told anyone. Not Lydia and Kiley, certainly not her parents, not even Jorge. She was too humiliated; would gladly have paid all the money she had saved from doing tattoos just to erase him from her memory. But since that was impossible, she was damn well going to move on with her life. He would never, ever, *ever* have the satisfaction of knowing how much he'd hurt her.

Which was why she and Jorge were on Pico Boulevard near Century City Plaza, riding up the elevator in a nondescript office building with Miranda Olsen from Tip-top Realtors. Miranda specialized in small-business commercial real estate, or so her ad in the Yellow Pages claimed. She was in her mid-thirties, Esme guessed, with strawberry blond curls, and skin so white that Esme noticed she had no hair on her forearms.

"It's the fourteenth floor," Miranda explained as she stabbed the number fourteen on the grid with one short, clear-nail-polished fingertip. "Actually it's the thirteenth, but they skipped that number because it's so unlucky." She tossed her hair off her face, sighed, and looked pointedly at her watch.

Great, Esme thought as she shifted her weight to ease her throbbing feet. The red suede pumps she'd bought at Shoe Show—"All Shoes Ten Dollars!"—were giving her blisters; she could actually feel them forming. This was the seventh place that the realtor had shown them. All Esme wanted was a decent space to rent for Skin Art, as she was thinking of calling her tattoo business.

Jonathan. Jonathan who?

Convincing Miranda that two brown-skinned teenagers with a business plan—fortunately Jorge was already eighteen years old—were serious about renting decent commercial real estate wasn't exactly Esme's forte. Miranda had started out showing them the crappiest places, such as a commercial building in Los Feliz with a rusting façade on the outside and garbage overflowing in the hallway.

Esme, who was still in a foul mood because of the J-word, had been ready to slap her for treating them as if she was doing them a favor. Fortunately, Jorge had intervened and charmed her into taking them here.

"And this space is going for five thousand a month," Miranda said as she led the way off the elevator and down the generic hallway.

Esme nearly gasped. Five thousand? A month?

She'd been thinking three thousand, tops. Who knew how many clients she'd have? And if she spent all her profit on rent, what was the point of taking the place at all?

Esme was ready to turn it down before even seeing the space, but Jorge squeezed her hand and cocked his head forward as if to say: *Let's at least look at it.*

They stepped into what was obviously a very small former dentist's office.

Miranda power-walked through the room, which didn't take long. She rattled off vitals at top speed. "Two electric dental chairs, two sinks, one small bathroom, counter space—I think it's perfect for you," she chirped. "What do you think?"

What did she think? The space was fine! Okay, it was in a generic building and it had zero hip factor. But that really didn't matter. Esme knew from Jonathan that some of the most important producers and stars with their own production companies had offices in nondescript buildings just like this one. It was a Hollywood thing.

But . . . five thousand dollars? How was she going to swing five thousand dollars?

Jorge smiled at the Realtor. "Why didn't you just show us this in the first place?"

"I thought we'd work our way up," Miranda replied, handing Esme a clipboard with a pen the color and weight of gold. Esme felt nearly Jonathan-having-sex-with-Tarshea-level nauseated at the thought of signing the lease.

"What about advertising, insurance, taxes?"

Answering as if she'd been expecting the question, Miranda said, "For now you should talk to the other tenants in the building about basic coverage and taxes. As for advertising, you can use the spot on the sign out front that Dr. Laramie used. He had this space before you," she added confidentially. "Ran away with the dental hygienist."

Esme looked at Jorge. He shrugged. "The space is great. You just have to know this is what you really want."

What did she really want? Her parents would be furious when she told them that she was dropping out of school—she hadn't let that bombshell fly yet. Did she really want to do that? She knew she didn't want to do senior year back in the Echo with the gangbangers and the gritty poverty. But she wanted to go to Bel Air High even less. So what the hell *did* she want?

Jonathan.

No, dammit. She did not want him. And she did not want to continue to work for his parents, where she would keep running into him when he came to see her roommate, Tarshea, and every single time it would be like opening the wound again.

Miranda rechecked her watch. "I really do have other appointments."

"Can I have a day or two to think about it?" Esme asked.

Miranda pulled the strap of her oversized white leather bag higher on her bony shoulder. "For the record, this place is a steal, so don't blame me if it's gone by the time you call," she replied.

When they reached the sidewalk, Miranda pressed yet another one of her cards into Jorge's hand and took off for the parking garage. When she was gone, Esme convinced Jorge to stop into a small café called Clementine next door to the office building, insisting it was her treat. They both ordered coffee and the muffin of the day—soy banana—and took it to a small table near the back.

"Let's not talk about the lease just yet. How does it feel to be living back home?" Jorge asked as he poured sugar into his coffee.

Esme thought for a minute. "Weird" was what she finally came up with. In some ways it made her feel like a failure. But that was crazy, since she was making sick *dinero*. But she could feel her mother's sad eyes on her all the time, could see the censure in the set of her father's tense mouth.

"It's hard for my parents," she added, her voice low.

"They want more for you."

Right. Esme already knew that. They thought she had blown the biggest opportunity of her life. She knew Jorge didn't agree with the changes she'd made, either, but he was too good of a friend to come right out and say so. Should she tell him about Jonathan? What if he just said, *I told you so,* chica? She would feel even more like shit than she already did.

"I didn't just decide to stop being a nanny because of the

money," Esme finally said. And then she told him about walking in on Jonathan and Tarshea.

"*No sabes que tienes hasta se va,*" Jorge murmured, sipping his coffee.

"You don't know what you've got till it's gone," she translated. "You mean you think I'm going to miss him now, eh?" She swore under her breath.

"I meant he was going to miss you," Jorge said gently. "And what about the twins? Adults keep walking in and out of their lives. How do you think they're gonna feel about you just disappearing?"

"They love Tarshea," Esme replied. "Diane loves Tarshea. Jonathan definitely loves Tarshea. It's a lovefest. No one will miss me."

"I don't believe that." Jorge bit into his muffin. The look on his face—somewhere between shock and disgust—made Esme crack up.

"It's bad?"

"The worst thing I ever tasted," Jorge managed, and he washed the bite of muffin down with a huge gulp of coffee.

Esme threw hers away. As they walked out of the café, Jorge looped a sinewy arm around her shoulders. "Just remember, *chica.* You can't run away from your problems."

"Do not do that psychologist bull with me," Esme warned.

"You got it," Jorge agreed. They reached the door. Before he held it open for her, he added, "If I can say just one more thing about it."

Esme folded her arms and gave him the evil eye. "Well? Go ahead."

"Wherever you go, Esme . . . there you are."

• • •

Tom opened the door to his suite at the Hotel Bel-Air sporting their logo-embroidered terry cloth bathrobe, which fell open to reveal his tanned washboard abs and a pair of faded, low-slung jeans.

"You look like a model," she accused, teasing him.

"Oh, I just play one on TV," he joked, and pulled her into a kiss. The kiss got hotter. She could feel Tom's hand inching under her T-shirt. And she liked it. A lot. But she stepped back and put a palm on his chest. "The recreation portion of the activities will have to wait."

"Until after you call your mom," Tom concluded. "Got it."

Kiley sat in the taupe Italian leather desk chair and pulled out her phone. "I so do not want to make this call." She had to try once more to clean up in the aftermath of the bomb that was the *Universe* exposé.

"What's the worst thing that can happen?" Tom asked, sitting on the edge of the bed.

"Thermonuclear war?" Kiley ventured. "Dragging me back to La Crosse by my ponytail?"

He yanked said ponytail playfully. "Just call."

Kiley pressed the speed-dial number. It rang three times before her mother answered.

"Hello?" Her mother sounded tentative, unsure, as if somehow even making the choice to answer the phone could turn out to be a bad thing.

Kiley did her best at sounding upbeat. "Hi, Mom!"

"Kiley? Oh, thank goodness. I thought it was one of those reporters again. Do you have any idea what your father and I have been dealing with?"

Kiley winced. She could imagine: reporters on the phone, on the doorstep, in the grocery store. Friends and coworkers during the hours in between. All asking too-well-informed questions about every private McCann vice. Jeanne's panic disorder, her father's drinking, the piece-of-crap house they lived in—a photo of which had been printed in the *Universe* right next to a photo of Platinum's mansion, with the caption THIS IS HOW FAR PLATINUM'S NANNY HAS COME.

"I can explain about the story, Mom."

"How could you do that?" her mother asked, voice tightening. "We raised you better."

Well, that one scored a big fat bull's-eye at the heart of Kiley's guilt.

"I'm sorry," Kiley said, and she truly was; she knew how badly she'd handled this. "It's just been crazy here. And I had really hoped that the sleazy guy who wrote the article wouldn't really print it—"

"Well, you thought wrong. They made us sound like horrible, stupid people. They said I had a nervous condition and they called your father an alcoholic!"

Well, um, her mother *did* have a nervous condition and her father *was* an alcoholic. But pointing out that this part of the article had been factual did not seem to be the way to go at the moment, especially since Kiley could hear the increased speed of her mother's raspy breathing, a sure sign she was heading straight for a panic attack.

Kiley tried to talk her down. "Just breathe, Mom. You're safe now. There's nothing to worry about."

"Kiley?" Her father's sandpaper voice rasped in Kiley's ear. He must have taken the phone from his wife.

181

Kiley closed her eyes. This was really, really not good.

"What?" Tom whispered.

"My father," Kiley mouthed at him. "Hi, Dad," she greeted him. "I know you—"

"Do you have any idea what you're putting your mother through?" he asked.

Now that she'd heard a complete sentence, she realized her father was slurring his words, meaning that he was already drunk.

"I'm sorry," Kiley said. "Things got out of control." Tom reached over and squeezed her hand.

"You're a snot-nosed brat, Kiley," he brayed. "Ungrateful little—"

"Give me the phone!" Kiley heard her mother exclaim.

"Shut up," her father hissed. "I'm gonna give her a piece of my mind."

Kiley felt as though she was about to have her own panic attack. "I admit I should have told you ahead of time," she said, careful to keep her voice even. "But I am not responsible for that article." She wanted to detail that she was blindsided too, that the *Universe* had manipulated her, that Platinum really *was* improving, and that technically, Kiley had made all the right decisions.

But her mother would hyperventilate way before Kiley could ever get through that story, and her father was too wasted to listen. Or care.

In fact, after braying at her for another five minutes, her father hung up on her. Just like that. Kiley was left with a dead phone in her hand, until Tom gently took her phone from her and put it on the desk.

"I should have told them." Kiley let the guilt wash over her as she stared unblinking at the Victorian-inspired molding on the ceiling.

"Come 'ere." Tom tugged her onto the bed with him. "Your parents will forgive you. As far as the Hollywood gossip mill goes, they're already onto the next thing, I guarantee it."

She leaned into him. "You're right. I just . . . I feel bad. Like I let them down."

"You're too hard on yourself." Tom used two fingers to bring her face to his and kissed her lightly. "You do not appreciate the Kiley I know." He kissed her again. "She is genuine, and sweet and smart and sexy because she doesn't try to be, in a town where that's about as rare as natural hair color."

Kiley laughed. "They gave me streaks during the TV show. I can't even claim—"

But she never finished the sentence. Because Tom's hand was tangled in her hair, his lips were burning into hers, and she never, ever wanted it to stop. This time she had no doubts, or insecurities, or fears that he was the gorgeous model and she was just some ordinary girl from Wisconsin.

She'd weathered the storm of Platinum's trial. She'd overcome her panic underwater. And she was here with Tom because that was what they both wanted.

When he tugged her T-shirt over her head, she didn't stop him.

"Yes?" he whispered, peering into her eyes.

"Yes," she said.

20

"So, when they say Up All Night, do you think they mean up all night as in sex? Or up all night as in we never went to sleep?" Lydia asked as Kiley pulled Platinum's new silver Prius (purchased, Kiley had told Lydia on the drive to Malibu, because she thought she'd get good publicity for it) into the line of cars leading to the temporary valet stand.

They were at the rear side of a massive beach house of unbleached wood; the front of the house faced the ocean and was not accessible by car. This beach house belonged to the parents of a girl in what would be their senior class at Bel Air High. Her name was Heidi Van Meussen. Her father, Alex Van Meussen, was the genius behind all the Pixar cartoon movies. Lydia knew this because she'd done her research before the party. According to an article she had unearthed in *Los Angeles* magazine, the Van Meussens owned homes in Bel Air, Malibu, and Hawaii, and had also recently purchased a castle in Scotland. Their Malibu beach house was "cozy," only ten thousand square feet, and was nestled between homes owned by Steven Spielberg and Barbra Streisand.

"I think it means what you want it to mean," Kiley replied as she inched the car closer to the valet stand.

Lydia flicked her eyes at her friend. "Not that you care, now that you and Tom are doin' it." Kiley had informed her of this on the way to Malibu too. Lydia wanted details, which Kiley refused to provide.

"Well, I doubt that you're going to jump some guy you just met on the sand," Kiley said. "But I have no idea what these other girls will do."

"I might jump two or three guys," Lydia mused as Kiley pulled the car up a little farther. "I've decided that variety is the spice and all that. I hooked up with Billy too soon. Now I just want to have fun."

Lydia found she actually meant it. Yes, she felt terrible about Billy. Yes, she had messed up. And yes, she missed him. But on the other hand, she had a lot of years of no-boys-at-all to make up for. Maybe she just wasn't cut out for a serious relationship right now. At least, that was the theory her mother had floated just this morning at breakfast.

Her mom also talked about going back to the Amazon again, which didn't surprise Lydia one bit. She knew that her mom's stay in L.A. would be temporary. Her parents loved each other too much to live apart.

Now, she peered out the window at the valet, who was holding open the door of the Jeep in front of them. "How tacky is that?" she asked rhetorically.

The valet attendants from Play Valet, which was *the* hot valet service of the moment, were all female and all gorgeous. They wore yellow bikinis and high heels. Lydia had nothing against either the bathing suits or the pumps. But to wear them so that you could hold open doors for people?

"Why did I come?" Kiley asked, drumming her fingers on the steering wheel. "I don't like any of the girls we've met at that school so far—"

"Well, that's why, sugar plum. Everyone in our class can't be a big ol' pile of puke like Staci, Amber, and Zona—finally!"

Kiley pulled the car up to the valet stand. A girl with jet black hair extensions down to her ass held open the car door. "Welcome to Up All Night!" she chirped. "Your car keys, please?" She handed Kiley a claim ticket and got in the car to drive it off to who-knows-where.

Lydia eyed Kiley as they headed down the wooden pathway that led around the house and down to the beach. "Are you wearing a bathing suit under your jeans?"

Kiley had on one of her usual outfits—no-name jeans and a white tank top—and her hair was in its habitual ponytail. "Nope."

"But it's a beach party," Lydia pointed out. She herself had on a hot pink crocheted Bizmark string bikini under a sheer pale pink lace babydoll top over low-slung D&G white capri jeans.

"Rag on me all you want for having body issues," Kiley said. "I am not wearing a bathing suit in front of a bunch of size twos."

"One of these days we are taking you swimsuit shopping," Lydia insisted. "And get something cute that shows off your curves." She smiled at a cute blond boy who swerved around them, then looked back at her with appreciation. "I bet Tom likes those curves."

Kiley smiled. "No, I am not telling you *anything*."

"Well, what kind of best friend are you?" Lydia groused. She saw one of the few Latina girls in their class walk by with her boyfriend. But that Latina girl was the daughter of a huge action-movie star. "It's weird, isn't it? That Esme isn't here?"

"I keep hoping she'll change her mind about dropping out of school."

"Me too."

They followed the hordes of other arriving seniors down the wooden steps to the beach. It was ablaze with tiki lights. A wooden dance floor had been set up in the sand; a DJ in a white tux minus a shirt was blasting the Red Hot Chili Peppers. Waiters in surfer Jams, the buff-male version of the girls who worked for the valet service, were wandering among the party guests with drinks and food.

Lydia and Kiley grabbed drinks—coconuts with some fruity concoction in them—from a passing waiter. Lydia could tell as soon as she took a sip that it was heavily laced with rum. She made a mental note not to drink too much. If she did meet somebody, she was going to know what the hell she was doing, and who the hell she was doing it with. No more drunk sex. *Ever.*

"Let's see what's going on over there." Lydia cocked her head toward a throng of people sitting on the beach farther down. Salty sea air whipped Lydia's hair into her face as they padded through the sand. When they got closer to the crowd, they saw that someone had placed a surfboard on the sand, and the people gathered around it were playing a drinking game.

"Ugh," Kiley whispered to Lydia.

"Well, if it isn't the bitch and her fat cheese-fried friend," Staci sneered, coming up next to Lydia and Kiley. She wore a white bikini and had clearly indulged in a serious spray-on tan.

"Now see, that is just a mean ol' thing to say," Lydia said. "I'm not a bitch and my friend here isn't fat. You, however, are really boring. Which is why I dumped your ass the other night. Also, you might want to find a new place to spray on your tan, because you're going kind of orange sunset on us."

Some kids who overheard snickered.

"Oh, like I'm hurt," Staci retorted. "Hey, do you know why these two are going to our school?" She raised her voice to the drinkers. "Because they're *nannies*! Isn't that a hoot?"

"You're an asshole, Staci," a cute guy with spiky black hair, intense blue eyes, and a perfect V-cut body called back. He scrambled up from the group just as the bottle was passed to a girl with pink streaks in her honey blond hair. She pointed to a guy with a blond crew cut and they started to make out in the center of the circle while the others cheered them on.

"Screw you," Staci spit at him.

"You're drunk," he told her. "Go puke."

Staci stormed away, giving them all the finger.

"Hey," the guy said, holding out a hand to Lydia. "I'm Flipper. And yeah, I know it's a stupid nickname," he added with a dimpled grin. "It's a swim-team thing."

Well, well. Things were looking up already.

"I'm Lydia." She shook his outstretched hand. "And this is my friend Kiley."

"There are only a handful of new seniors," Flipper explained.

"Most of us have known each other forever. It's great to see some new faces." Flipper shook Lydia's hand, and then Kiley's. "So you guys are really nannies?"

"You probably recognize Kiley. She's Platinum's nanny—"

"I knew you looked familiar!" Flipper exclaimed.

This got the attention of others in the group, who turned to assess Kiley anew. Pretty soon a small group surrounded her, asking all kinds of questions about Platinum and the trial.

"Platinum's a total drug addict, right?" a pixieish girl asked Kiley eagerly.

"I . . . don't really like to talk about my employer," Kiley said carefully.

"Oh wait, I saw that article about you in the *Universe*," a pretty girl with perfect skin and blue eyes exclaimed.

Some other kids started saying they had seen it too.

If they started ragging on Kiley because she came from a working-class family, or because her dad was an alcoholic or for anything else they read in that gossip rag, Lydia was fully prepared to put a blow dart into the butt of the nearest ass.

However, instead of making fun of Kiley, kids were fascinated. They kept asking her questions about Platinum and what it was like for Kiley to live with her.

That was when Lydia had the ironic realization that no matter how rich people were, they were all still obsessed with anything having to do with fame. By virtue of the article in the *Universe*, Kiley had been rendered cool to the cool kids of Bel Air High.

Flipper playfully bumped into Lydia. "Hey." He offered a winning smile. "Do you swim?"

"I'm not real big on the water, frankly," Lydia admitted. "But I can swing from a vine like Tarzan and cook monkey over an open pit."

Flipper's jaw fell open.

"She's a very interesting girl," Kiley put in on her behalf.

"So I see." Flipper offered his killer grin again. "You want to join the game?" He cocked his head toward the group, which had set down a bottle of Cuervo Gold to play spin the bottle.

"No!" Kiley said at the same time that Lydia said, "Love to!"

"If you don't want to, I won't either," Lydia insisted. "We can go get something to eat. Or do something else that would be a lot more boring than playing a kissing game with Flipper here."

Flipper laughed. "I like your style."

"See, the thing is, Kiley here just had sex with her boyfriend for the first time," Lydia confided. "So she's not in the mood to swap spit with anyone else."

"Lydia!" Kiley gasped as Flipper cracked up. "Fine. I'll play. Just don't . . . talk about my personal life!"

"Deal," Lydia said sweetly. She put her hand in Flipper's. "Count us in," she said.

An hour later, Lydia was making out with Flipper. Kiley edged away from the spin the bottle game—fortunately, she hadn't gotten a turn because the public make-out sessions on the surfboard tended to go on for a long time while the crowd egged them on. When one girl picked another girl to kiss—it was clear to Kiley by the way they kept eyeing the guys watching them that they were doing it for attention and not because they were actually gay—she scrambled up and left to get something to eat. The food was amazing: a dozen varieties of miniburgers no bigger than the palm of her hand, twenty different kinds of sushi, and cold poached lobster served on avocado.

After that, she took a walk by herself down the beach, feeling oddly content. She had been so worried about that horrible article in the *Universe*. And yes, it had hurt her parents, but they'd get over it. As far as her own life went, because of all the media attention surrounding Platinum's life—the article on Kiley included—she was now being treated like a reality-TV star.

And because of that, suddenly, *she* was cool.

Kiley was far enough away so that she could only faintly hear the tunes the DJ was spinning. She let her shoes dangle from two fingers and padded along in her bare feet. The briny air bit at her; she inhaled deeply, loving the smell, the salty feel of it. She knelt and picked up a shell and threw it into a breaking wave.

Her cell rang. She reached into her back pocket and took it out, checking caller ID. And smiled.

"Hi."

"Hi, yourself," came Tom's deep, sexy voice. It made her think of what had happened the night before. She had finally taken the plunge; it had been incredible, fantastic. *He* was incredible, fantastic.

"Whatcha doing?" Tom asked. His voice was low, teasing.

"Watching the ocean."

"How's the Up All Night party?"

Late the night before, when she'd lain in his arms, she'd told him about the unofficial start-of-senior-year party, how she planned to go with Lydia. Tom said it sounded like fun.

But now? Now she knew better.

"The party's okay," she replied, curling her toes into the sand. "Lydia found a guy."

Tom laughed. "Why does that not surprise me?"

"Me either," Kiley admitted.

"You staying late?"

"Hey, up all night as advertised," Kiley said.

"I could keep you up all night," he offered. "Well, let me amend that. You could keep *me* up all night."

If he'd been able to see her at that moment, he would have seen the happy blush on her face. It had been amazing how, once she decided she really, truly wanted to make love with him, for all the right reasons, she hadn't felt self-conscious at all.

"Hey, I got some great news today," he said. "Well, it's not for sure yet. . . ."

She smiled at the boyish enthusiasm in his voice. "What? I love great news."

"I've been up for a part in this high-profile indie film—a college student gets framed for murder—my agent says he thinks I got it."

"The lead?" Kiley exclaimed. "That is so fantastic!"

"Second lead," Tom said. "I'd play his best friend, who turns out to be a bad guy. I don't feel like I even know how to act yet—"

"But you were so good in *The Ten*," Kiley insisted. "And the director must feel confident or he wouldn't cast you."

"She," Tom corrected.

"She, then. And I'm ticked at myself for just assuming it's a guy."

"I should get the actual offer, like, tomorrow or the next day," Tom went on. "So cross your fingers and toes for me."

"All appendages are now officially crossed," Kiley said. "When would it start shooting?"

"In two weeks. They're fast-tracking it to get the female lead they want. They're shooting in Moscow."

Wait. She couldn't possibly have heard that correctly. "Did you say . . . Moscow? Like in Russia, Moscow?"

"That's the one," Tom said.

"How long would you be in Moscow?"

"Three months, maybe a little more to rehearse," Tom replied.

No. This couldn't be happening. He was giving her this information as if he was telling her he was shooting a movie in, say, Santa Barbara, and she'd be able to come see him or he could come see her all the time.

Not a word about how far away it was.

Not a word about how much he'd miss her.

Hey! I gave you my virginity last night and now you're going to freaking Moscow? Kiley felt like screaming. But he already knew that.

And at the moment, it didn't seem to matter to him at all.

21

"What would you like, Esme?"

Esme knew the waitress at La Verdad. Her name was Marlene and she'd been a classmate of Esme's at Echo Park High School. They hadn't been friends there, but they hadn't been enemies either. She was very tall for a Latina girl—easily five foot ten, and willow-thin. If she'd grown up in Bel Air or Beverly Hills, she could have been a model. Instead, she was helping her parents make ends meet by waitressing here at the biggest neighborhood hang in the Echo.

"Bring me a *horchata*, Marlene. A really big *horchata*. If you got some." Esme named the famous summertime rice-based drink that quenched a thirst better than any soda or even beer. Esme knew that every morning, the owner of La Verdad—*the truth,* in Spanish—mixed a ten-gallon batch of *horchata* in his kitchen, and it rarely lasted the day.

"I think there's a little left. If there is, it's got your name on it." Marlene made to move off, then hesitated. "Esme, can I ask you something?"

"Sure."

"That time you were over in Bel Air?"

"Yeah?"

Marlene frowned. "Did you lose your mind, or what? Because down here, we all thought you went out of your mind."

Esme was about to explain. But how could she? To start at the beginning would take all night.

"I'll tell you another time, Marlene. Can you check on that *horchata* for me?"

"Sure thing."

The waitress moved off, and Esme was alone again. Back when she used to live in the Echo, she'd come to La Verdad all the time. This was the place where Jorge's group, the Latin Kings, loved to perform the most. It was the Echo equivalent of Starbucks, but with so much more character. If Starbucks was liberal, La Verdad was communist. There were posters of Che Guevara, César Chávez, and Fidel Castro on the walls, along with bellicose anticapitalist graffiti. During the pro-immigration marches, when hundreds of thousands of Latinos marched through downtown Los Angeles calling for a sane American immigration policy that would take undocumented workers out of the shadows, La Verdad had been an impromptu organizational center. Esme could still remember the huge crowds of demonstrators that gathered in front of La Verdad, listening to Spanish-radio DJs like El Piolin psych them up for the long walk into downtown.

It was already ten o'clock, and the place was crowded with its usual assortment of neighborhood types on a night when there was no entertainment. One of the local Spanish-language radio stations played over the sound system; there were gatherings of middle-aged men in jeans and work shirts playing dominos in clusters around the room; plus a few couples, groups of younger teenagers, and even a few *abuelas* chattering happily in Spanish. That was nice. But it wasn't surprising. Jorge loved to remind Esme that Los Angeles was now more than fifty percent Latino and—

Esme froze. Because a very non-Latino young guy had just walked in the door. He stopped at the entrance and looked around uncertainly. No one paid him any mind at all, though a lone white guy in La Verdad was a rarity. Still, since he was alone, he wouldn't cause any trouble. Probably just a motorist who'd gotten lost.

But Esme knew better. This was no handsome lost motorist. It was Jonathan Goldhagen. There could be only one reason that he was here at La Verdad, and it wasn't the delicious *horchata*.

"Esme? Here's your *horchata*." Marlene set the frothy white glass topped with flecks of hand-chopped cinnamon—they didn't mess around in the La Verdad kitchen—in front of her.

"Thanks."

Jonathan still stood there, his eyes sweeping the room. As he did, Esme made a decision.

"Marlene? Can you do me a favor? You see that gringo standing in the doorway looking like he doesn't belong here, because he doesn't?"

Marlene peered across the room. "The fine guy?"

"I think I know him. Can you go over there and point out where I'm sitting? I got a feeling he's looking for me."

"You sure?" Marlene looked dubious.

"Of course I'm sure. I wouldn't be asking otherwise."

That was enough to get Marlene headed across the floor of the coffeehouse. Esme saw her have a brief conversation with Jonathan, put her hand on his arm, and point right at her.

She expected Jonathan's face to light up when he saw her. It didn't. Instead, it was a mask of grim determination. Meanwhile, she had so many conflicting feelings, and conflicting questions. Should she have told Marlene to tell him to go to hell? How did Jonathan even find her? She'd put every number from the Goldhagens' mansion on block, including every cell phone she could remember. Including Jonthan's cell. So in the days since she had resigned from her job at the Goldhagens'— they'd accepted her resignation immediately, and transmitted the news via her parents—she had no idea whether Jonathan had even called her. Part of her hoped he had. Part of her wished he hadn't.

Now, here he was. Dressed in jeans and a blue tennis shirt, he'd trimmed his hair to short and spiky. But his tan was darker, as if he'd been spending a lot of time in the sun or on the beach. Why shouldn't he? He had that great apartment in Santa Monica.

His first words were a brief question. "May I?"

Her answer was a sweep of her hand toward the battered wooden upright chair across from her. His answer to that was to sit and put his elbows on the equally battered wooden table. "I'm glad you'll talk to me. You look great."

"Bullshit. I look like a girl in the Echo." This was true. Esme had worn nothing special to come to La Verdad. Just a pair of jeans and a black tank top.

"That's great."

"Forget it, Jonathan. I don't want compliments from you. How'd you find me?"

He shrugged. "I called your mom. She said you weren't home but might be at this place. I took a chance. I'm glad I did. I remember this place from the time we came to hear your friend Jorge and his group. The fire department closed it down because there were too many people."

Esme took a sip of the *horchata,* and wiped the white line she was sure it made away from her upper lip. She remembered that time, too. That was when she and Jonathan were an actual couple.

"She shouldn't have."

"You'll have to take that up with her. What are you drinking?"

She deliberately hit herself in the forehead three or four times before she answered. "Come on, Jonathan. You didn't drive out here to the Echo—or did you have one of the drivers bring you?—just to find out what I'm drinking."

He put his palms up. "Guilty as charged."

"Anyway, it's *horchata.* A rice drink. If you want, get my friend Marlene to bring you some."

"Not thirsty. I came to see you."

She shrugged. "Cool. Here I am. Talk. I think you probably have something you've planned to say. Say it. I promise I won't move until you're done."

"What about after that?"

"Jonathan. Don't push your luck."

The radio station music changed to something by Santana—and Esme had a brief flash to that day not long ago when she'd come back to the mansion to find Tarshea making genuine Jamaican jerk chicken, and her feeling like a genuine jerk. Then there was the water volleyball game afterward, when Santana had been in the pool along with Jonathan and Tarshea, and all she could do was stand on the sideline and watch. That had been close to humiliating.

Maybe Jonathan had the same memory. His eyes clouded over.

"What are you thinking about?" she demanded.

"You don't really want to know."

"If I didn't want to know, I'd change my mind and leave. Which is what maybe I should do if I had any sense." She was getting aggravated. Maybe the best thing to do was to go home and tell her mother never, ever to tell this guy where she was.

"Fine. I was thinking about when you showed up at my door. And Tarshea was inside."

"Oh," Esme mocked. "What a nice memory."

"I want to tell you something about that night. It wasn't what it looked like."

Esme laughed in a way that wasn't funny. "Do you realize that's the oldest line in the book? What do you take me for? A dumb girl FOB? Fresh off the boat?"

"It's the truth." Jonathan defended himself. "It wasn't what it looked like."

"Then why don't you tell me what it was?" Esme knew her voice was cutting, but she didn't care. She'd never been in the habit of letting guys take advantage of her, and she wasn't about to start now. On the other hand, she was curious to see what kind of lame-ass excuse Jonathan would concoct.

"Here's what happened. I was home. I heard my buzzer. It was her, downstairs. She sounded totally polluted. I let her in. She *was* polluted. Seriously drunk. We didn't do anything. I mean it, Esme. Nothing."

Esme just sat there for a minute, thinking. It was bullshit. It wasn't bullshit. It was bullshit.

It was bullshit.

"You were in your bathrobe!"

Jonathan's response was instantaneous. "Because she'd just barfed all over me."

"Prove it," she challenged.

"I can't."

"Knew it."

"I would if I could," Jonathan said. "But I can't. Since Tarshea has gone back to Jamaica."

Well then. For the first time since Jonathan had sat down at her table, Esme felt surprised by something he'd said. This couldn't be bullshit. It was too easy to check. But if that was the case, why hadn't her parents told her?

The answer was self-evident, even as he looked at her expectantly, waiting for her reaction. She'd made it so clear she didn't give a rat's ass about what was happening at the Goldhagen estate that they'd adopted their own bilingual don't-ask, don't-tell policy. That had to be why.

"When?" Esme asked.

"After I told my folks that she showed up at my place drunk," Jonathan explained.

"Nice. You cost Tarshea her job."

"No, Esme. Tarshea cost Tarshea her job. Now, my parents have no one. The girls have no one."

He looked at her with those deep-set eyes, and for a moment she felt herself back under his spell.

But no. That was an Esme who was no more. Since that

200

night, everything had changed. She'd decided not to be a nanny. To be a tattoo artist instead. To make the kind of money and have the kind of business that would give her the kind of financial security she'd never had, and even security for her parents. She'd done the late-night calculations. Even with rent on her office space, even with buying the car she'd need to get back and forth and to do the occasional home visit (if it was safe, of course), she'd be in a position to make a down payment on a house inside of eighteen months.

Not for herself. For her parents. To get them out of the Echo, and into South Pasadena or Alhambra. Someplace where Spanish was still the first language, but where you heard the LAPD midnight sirens and choppers a lot less often.

"You should have told me right away." She could feel herself biting her lower lip. It was a nervous habit from when she was younger. She hadn't done it in ages.

"Maybe. But you'd quit. My parents were pissed."

"I was pissed," Esme retorted.

"It left them with no one. They've been using a service, but the twins are flipping out."

"I'm sorry to hear that." That was no exaggeration.

"So I'm here for two reasons." Jonathan puffed some air loudly between his lips. "One, to see if you'd be willing to talk to my parents about coming back."

"Does Diane know about this?" Esme interjected, before Jonathan could get to his second point.

He shook his head. "I thought I'd sound you out first."

This was it. A moment of decision. She knew it. He was basically offering to run interference for her in case she wanted her job back. But so much had changed. Working with those twins for a relative pittance seemed so long ago. Was she ready to roll back the clock?

"What's the other thing?"

"You're dodging," he said. "You answer the first one, I'll answer the second."

She couldn't help it. She smiled for a brief instant. "This is my turf. I'll decide."

"Fair enough. Decide on your own time." He stood. "But you should know that my stepmom said you had a week. Otherwise, she's going to go to the club and poach someone's nanny."

"Hold it." She stood too. "I thought you just told me that you hadn't talked to Diane and Steven about this."

He shrugged. "Sue me. I lied. Anyway, I gotta get back. I promised the twins I'd take them out for ice cream."

"At this hour?" She looked skeptical.

"Got me again. Anyway, the stuff about Diane saying you had a week? That's no lie. You know where to find her. And you know where to find me."

That was it. Twenty seconds later, the door of La Verdad swung shut behind him.

Marlene was on Esme in a minute. *"¿Oye, quién fue el chico? ¡Wow! ¡Muy lindo!"*

"Yeah, he's fine," Esme agreed. "The problem is, I don't know what he is after that."

22

"I just wanted to tell you," Susan began, looking deep into Kiley's eyes, "how relieved I am that you'll be here for the kids after the colonel and I are gone."

They were standing in front of the house. The colonel was supervising as the chauffeur put their packed bags in the limo's trunk. Although Platinum's sister made it sound as if she was dying, what with her dramatic *after the colonel and I are gone* thing, in actuality Kiley knew that she and her anal-retentive husband were simply moving out and moving on.

Bruce, Sid, and Serenity were about as happy as three kids could possibly be. At the moment, Bruce was off with his friends riding dirt bikes, Sid was in their home theater eating junk food and watching Johnny Knoxville movies, and Serenity was in her room with what had formerly been a black leather skirt of Platinum's, which she was cutting into clothing for her Barbie doll. Platinum herself was out at a *Rolling Stone* photo shoot.

No one in the entire family had bothered to show up to say goodbye.

Kiley felt kind of bad about that. She truly loathed the colonel. And she thought Susan was a wuss who refused to stand up for herself. But they had stepped into the breach after Platinum had screwed up her life and the lives of her children. Not to get a thank-you for it? That was cold.

Kiley waved as the limo disappeared out the privacy gate. And that was that.

"Kiley, dear. Can I get you some lunch?"

Kiley turned to see Mrs. Cleveland had come in from the kitchen.

"No thanks. I'm meeting my friends."

Kiley hesitated. She'd asked Platinum for the afternoon off so that she could hang out with Esme and Lydia. Esme was trying to decide whether or not she wanted her nanny job back, so her hours were her own. Lydia's aunt Kat had taken Jimmy and Martina to San Francisco for a much-needed sit-down with Anya on neutral ground after Anya had left several messages about needing to see the kids, and a deeply hurt Kat realized that she needed to put aside her anger to do what was best for them. Which meant Kiley was the only one who had been scheduled to work. Platinum had easily agreed. But Kiley was now so concerned that something terrible would happen with the kids if she wasn't there, she hated to leave.

"If you're sure about staying with the kids . . ."

"Of course." Mrs. Cleveland waved away Kiley's concerns. "Go have fun."

Kiley went back to her guesthouse, put on her well-worn Converse All Stars, a pair of shorts, and a T-shirt, and took off in

Platinum's pearl white Bentley for the spot where Esme had dictated they all meet—at the very end of Beachwood Canyon Drive in the Hollywood Hills. Kiley had MapQuested the driving directions. She had no idea why Esme had asked her and Lydia to meet at this location.

Enjoying this particular car's smooth ride, she was delighted to avoid the freeways and took local winding streets to this intriguing choice of location. She traveled upward on Beachwood Canyon, past beautiful homes that resembled the French countryside more than Los Angeles; Kiley found it charming. As she crossed such streets as Glen Holly, Glen Oak, and Cheremoya, the houses gave way to rolling green hills, and then . . . the street ended.

Esme had picked up Lydia. They'd already arrived; they were sitting on the bumper of a very used, very old maroon Saturn with a Latin Kings bumper sticker on the fender. Lydia had her head thrown back, face raised to the bright afternoon sun.

"Hey," Kiley called to them. "Interesting place to meet."

"I don't get it any more than you do, sweet pea," Lydia said, lifting her oversized sunglasses to make eye contact. "Just something Esme got into her head."

"It's actually something I've always wanted to do," Esme countered.

Lydia cocked one blond eyebrow. "Park at the end of a street in the Hollywood Hills?"

"We are not there yet, smart-ass," Esme informed her. "We have to walk. That way." She pointed to a dirt path that led upward.

"Sorry, but I left traipsing in the hot sun behind with the mud hut and fire ants," Lydia said.

Kiley saw Esme set her jaw. "Fine. You don't want to come—"

"We'll come," Kiley said quickly. "Won't we?" She made pointed eye contact with Lydia. Ever since Esme had quit her nanny job, she'd been . . . what? Kiley considered for a moment. Sad. That was it. She was sad. Not that she admitted it. She claimed that her life was perfect and she was glad to be rid of all things Goldhagen, but Kiley felt that in Esme's heart, she didn't really feel that way at all.

Which meant . . . that Esme really needed her friends right now. Esme never asked either of them for anything; Kiley always got the feeling that asking was a hard thing for Esme to do.

Lydia sighed. "Fine. But just so you know, I'm wearing four-hundred-dollar Chanel ballet flats, which were not made for hiking."

Kiley looked down at Lydia's shoes. "Please tell me you didn't pay four hundred dollars for those."

"Of course not," Lydia said primly. "I'm a *nanny*. I'm *broke*. My new friend Flipper bought them for me."

"Swimming guy, senior class, great kisser, washboard abs," Esme recited. "Although I don't know why you're letting some guy you just met buy you shoes."

"Well, see, Flipper turned eighteen last week," Lydia explained, clearly unbothered by Esme's criticism. "His real generous parents—they own this bathing suit empire—gave him his inheritance. Twenty-something million."

"You're kidding," Kiley said.

"If I'm lying, I'm dying," Lydia sang out. "To not let a boy with that kind of change buy me one little pair of shoes seemed downright criminal."

Kiley had to laugh. One thing about Lydia—she could always make Kiley laugh.

As they made their way up the steep narrow path and Kiley began to huff and puff, she noticed that Lydia, even in her non-climbing-friendly four-hundred-dollar shoes, was moving forward like a freaking gazelle. Esme filled them in on the fact that Jonathan had come to her, claiming he had not had sex with Tarshea at all, that in fact she'd shown up at his place drunk. And that his stepmother had fired Tarshea, who was already back in Jamaica.

Kiley was amazed. Was it possible that Jonathan hadn't really cheated on Esme? "Do you think he was telling you the truth?"

"I don't know and I don't care," Esme insisted.

"Liar, liar, pants on fire," Lydia sang out. "Hey, what is this mountain we're climbing, anyway?"

"Mount Lee," Esme replied. "And we're almost to the top."

"What's at the top?" Kiley called up to her.

"You'll see," Esme called back.

Finally, they came to a fence. Above the fence was a ring of security cameras. Kiley smiled, because she now realized where they were, even if she didn't know why they were there. Behind the fencing was the fifty-foot-high Hollywood sign.

"The Hollywood sign!" Lydia exclaimed, delighted. "Dang, girl, I would never have expected you to take us to the Hollywood sign. I know all about this place. The sign was put up something like eight decades ago and it originally said Hollywoodland, to advertise some new apartment complex."

"Don't tell me you read that in the Amazon," Kiley said.

"Did too. *Vogue* did a photo shoot and got permission to

actually use the sign. It used to be lit up with something like four thousand lightbulbs. And let's see, what else . . . some actress jumped off the H and killed herself." She blanched. "You weren't planning to off yourself, I hope."

"Of course not," Esme replied. She leaned her back against the fence. Kiley watched emotions flit across her face. "This sign? It meant something to me. A world so far away from the Echo it might as well be Mars."

Kiley nodded, feeling terrible for Esme, who no longer had a job that put her inside that world.

"Diane asked me to come back and work for them," Esme said quietly. The edge of her mouth ticked upward. "She even offered me a raise."

"Tattoos pay a whole lot better," Lydia pointed out.

"That's not what's important!" Kiley insisted. "If you go back to the Goldhagens, you can do senior year at Bel Air High with us, and go to college, and . . . if you want the high life, you can earn it for yourself."

"I can earn it doing tattoos," Esme said angrily. "Ain't nothing magical about the Goldhagens." She turned to face the fence, lacing her fingers through it, staring out and up at that giant sign. "It feels just like this at the Goldhagens'. Like everything huge and magical and rich is just out of my reach. But I'll always be behind a fence. I'll never belong there."

"Well, hell's bells, girl, none of the three of us belongs there!" Lydia exclaimed.

"You do," Kiley reminded her. "You were born on the other side of this fence."

Lydia didn't say anything. She knew it was true just as much as they did.

"Tom's going to Russia," Kiley said softly. She hadn't told them yet, as if saying it out loud would make it more true. Yesterday, Tom had called to tell her that the offer for the movie had been made. That he'd be leaving for Russia in ten days. Kiley hadn't seen him since the night they'd made love. He didn't seem to be in any particular hurry to see her. It was almost as if what they'd done together—which was such a huge thing for her—had never even happened. Or as if it simply didn't mean to him what it meant to her.

Leaning against that fence, staring up at the sign, Kiley told her friends all of this. She felt tears form but willed them away.

"Okay, well, you'll miss him," Lydia agreed. "But he'll be back."

"You don't even get it," Esme said, the words hard in her mouth. "Kiley gave him something precious. He's treating it like it's *ninguna cosa grande,* no big thing."

"Admittedly, I didn't consider it so grand when I did it," Lydia said. "I'm just saying maybe you're reading more into it than you should, sweet pea."

"And maybe I'm not," Kiley countered. "Look, I can't tell you what to do, Esme. But if you want my opinion . . . ?"

"Yeah," Esme finally said.

"Your tattoo talent isn't going anywhere. But if you quit school now, you'll probably never go back. Never go to college. And I realize college isn't *everything,*" she added hastily. "But it kind of is to your parents."

Kiley wondered if she was about to go too far with what she was about to say. What the hell. She was going to say it anyway.

"No matter how much money you make, Esme, if you don't go back and finish what you started, I think you'll spend your whole life feeling like you're still behind this fence."

It was quiet for a long time. Finally Esme mumbled, "I have to think about it some more. Jorge wants me to go back," she added, almost as an afterthought.

"He's in love with you," Lydia said. "You know that, right?"

"Kind of," Esme admitted.

"Well, do you want to jump his bones or be his buddy?" Lydia probed.

Esme shrugged.

Lydia sighed. "You don't give a girl a lot to go on."

"Diane gave me a week to decide," Esme said.

Lydia smiled slyly. "Did Jorge give you a week, too?"

Esme laughed. "No. All I know is, I can't be with Jonathan. Whenever I'm with him, I feel like I'm trying to sneak into a country where I don't belong. No matter how I feel about him, or how much I think I want him, I can't live like that anymore."

"Maybe you should give yourself a week on that decision, too," Kiley ventured.

"Okay, y'all, how about this," Lydia said. "One week from to-day we meet right back here at the sign. Esme tells us what she decided." She pointed at Kiley. "You tell us if Tom is a good guy who got a great job offer, or he used you and he's lower than a pregnant duck. And I'll tell y'all just what Flipper can do with his . . . flipper!"

Kiley cracked up. There was really no one like Lydia.

They agreed to meet, one week from that very moment, at the exact same spot.

As they climbed down the hill, Kiley was lost in thought. She really had much more in common with Esme than she did with Lydia, in certain ways. She didn't feel as though she belonged in the rarefied world in which she now found herself any more than Esme did. Maybe she just hid it better.

But she did know this much. Whatever happened with Platinum—who could start doing drugs again at any moment; and whatever happened with Tom—who might not care about her nearly as much as she cared about him—some way, somehow, Kiley would find her own way to the other side of that fence.

She impetuously tugged on a hunk of Esme's hair, recalling a phrase Jorge had taught her when she'd briefly lived in the Echo herself.

"*Mi vida loca*," Kiley said.

Esme smiled. "Yeah. My crazy life, too."

"Right back atcha, sweet pea!" Lydia called as she led the way down the hill. "It's a crazy-ass life, but someone's got to live it! I guess that's the three of us."

Kiley found herself laughing with her friends all the way down the hill.

About the Author

Raised in Bel Air, Melody Mayer is the oldest daughter of a fourth-generation Hollywood family and has outlasted countless nannies.

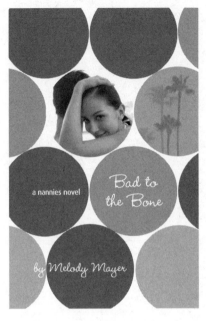

Bad to the Bone

a nannies novel

coming December 2008